P9-CDW-837

Stallion of the Desert

Stallion of the Desert

KELMAN FROST

Illustrated by Charles Pickard

ABELARD-SCHUMAN
London · New York · Toronto

By the same author:

EXILES IN THE SAHARA

First published 1966
Library of Congress Catalogue Card Number 66:10156
Printed in Great Britain by
Western Printing Services Ltd, Bristol

LONDON
Abelard-Schuman
Limited
8 King Street WC2

NEW YORK
Abelard-Schuman
Limited
6 West 57 Street

TORONTO
Abelard-Schuman
Canada Limited
896 Queen Street West

CONTENTS

PUBLISHER'S NOTE

This story is set in Algeria a few years ago, at a time when the country was under French rule. There was a strong underground force working for independence, and arms were frequently smuggled in from the borders of Tunisia and Morocco, which were already independent states. Algeria was granted independence in 1962.

1 A Dream Comes True

Aly sighed enviously as he watched the rider carefully descend the steep side of the wadi.

A well-built Arab boy of fourteen, he was keeping an eye on four camels as they drank at the waterhole. Barefooted, he wore a patched but clean cotton robe that came little more than past his sturdy knees. His arms were bare, for he had a hard day's work before him. On his head was a red tarboosh, which he wore pushed back from his brown, cheerful face, notable only for the high cheek bones and the firm mouth.

Aly ben Rabah was his full name, Aly the Son of Rabah, and he was a native of Yelten, a tiny oasis on the northern edge of the Sahara Desert.

His father had been the keeper of the *fondouk*, which meant he had looked after the enclosure in which travellers left their horses, camels, donkeys, and other beasts when passing through or visiting Yelten for the weekly market. Now that Rabah was dead Aly worked in the same *fondouk*, where he helped with the animals and ran errands for his father's successor. His earnings were pitifully small, but they were very important to his family, which was exceedingly poor.

The man on the horse was Sidi Ramdan ben Mizan, the local Caid, and the ruler of Yelten. It was not his wealth or position that Aly envied, but his Arab stallion.

Aly's greatest ambition was to own a horse. He loved horses, and he had ridden ever since he had been big enough to climb on to the back of a borrowed mount. When he was on a good horse he felt a different person, someone who would be able to face life and make a success of it. At such times he forgot his humble origin, the poverty of his family, and the certainty that he was destined to become a camel driver like his crippled brother. He felt capable of anything.

But what was the good of thinking like that? He would never own a horse, not even the sorriest specimen. The only time he would be able to ride would be when he took some traveller's mount to the water.

His eyes glowed as he watched the ripple of muscles under the satin skin of the Caid's stallion as it cautiously negotiated the last slope onto the ancient river bed. It was pure white, with a flowing mane, and a tail which touched its heels on the rare occasions when it drooped. Usually that superb tail was carried high, well arched, or streamed out behind it in the wind of its swift progress.

Aly knew that it was called Okba, and that it was a pure-blooded *asil*. He also knew that the Caid had paid a fabulous price for the stallion when he had imported it from Arabia. To Aly Okba was the most glorious sight in the whole of North Africa. He wished he could get work at the Caid's stable so that he might groom it, and worship it at close quarters.

It was not long after sunrise, and he was surprised that the Caid was astir so early. He guessed that he was going to visit the camps of some of the nomads who grazed their sheep at the foot of the Aurès Mountains.

The old river bed was dotted with small boulders and clumps of tough thorn bushes. Once a broad stream had flowed between those high banks, but centuries earlier the river had gone underground, as so many had done in the desert, and now the only indication that water was near was the coarse vegetation that grew among the boulders, and the waterhole which was such a boon to Yelten. It was the only place where it had not been necessary to sink wells to reach the water. Without water the oasis would never have come into being.

"Peace be with you, Aly ben Rabah!" called the Caid, when he was still some fifty paces distant. He was a kindly man, a just ruler, and knew the name of nearly everyone in Yelten.

"And with you be peace, Sidi!" replied Aly, standing respectfully to let him pass.

Sidi Ramdan ben Mizan was a short, thickset man, with a neat black beard. He wore baggy pantaloons tucked into boots of gazelle skin, and a short cotton jacket over a simple shirt. Only his headdress was more elaborate than that of most of his subjects. It was a turban made in three separate pieces; the *gannoure*, a high framework made of felt on which was wound the white silk *shesh*, the ends of which framed the wearer's face and tucked inside his coat. Strands of gold cord were interwoven with the *shesh*, and were called the *kheite*.

The Caid always dressed simply, except when he made one of his rare visits to Algiers or Constantine. He took no interest in politics, and devoted himself to the well-being of the several hundred peaceful folk who lived in Yelten, and to those who grazed their flocks in winter over his wide-spread desert territory.

He was almost level with Aly when it happened. There was a movement in the wiry grass which grew in a fringe about the pool, and something hurtled into the air, just missing the horse's chest. It was a horned-viper, small but deadly, and much feared by desert dwellers, for it attacked without reason and could leap as high as a man on horse-back.

Okba reared, screeching, and at the same time spun on his hind legs. The Caid, normally a superb rider, had been about to stop to talk further with the boy, and he had not been gripping with his knees. Taken completely by surprise, he fell backwards out of the saddle, and landed heavily in the sand. His turban was jolted from his head and fell in the grass several yards away.

In another moment Okba would have bolted, but Aly sprang in and gripped the bridle, hanging on with all his weight and strength as the stallion squealed and fought.

Round and round the boy was dragged, sometimes with his feet clear of the ground, until finally his soothing voice and tenacity calmed the frightened animal, and it became still, snorting through blood-red nostrils and rolling its eyes as they sought the snake, which had now disappeared into the scrub.

For the first time Aly looked at the Caid, who had risen to his feet, badly shaken, dusty, his bald head glistening in the sunlight. It was not the sight of the bleeding scratches on his face which caused Aly to cry out in dismay. It was the man's expression, and the revolver which he had whipped out from somewhere on his person.

Kindly and just though he was, Sidi Ramdan ben Mizan had inherited a vicious temper. His rare rages were discussed in whispers by those who had witnessed them, but Aly had never seen him in this mood, and was shocked.

"Hold the brute still!" growled the Caid, raising the revolver. "No horse which behaves like that shall have a place in my stable."

Aly saw that he was trying to take aim at the middle of Okba's forehead, where one shot would cause instant death.

With a strength he had not known he possessed, he swung the horse around so that its flank was to the Caid, and, holding onto the reins, jumped forward to be between the animal and the levelled gun.

"No, no, Sidi, do not shoot!" he protested. "You cannot shoot Okba. He is beautiful—the most beautiful horse

in Africa. It was not his fault. You must not shoot him!"

He had turned very pale, but his eyes blazed as he faced the revolver. He would have preferred that the bullet hit him rather than end the life of the magnificent animal which breathed so heavily at his side.

For a moment he thought that Ramdan ben Mizan would pull the trigger. Then the anger died slowly from the Caid's face. He lowered the revolver and thrust it into a hidden holster beneath his jacket.

"You are a brave boy, Aly!" he said, quietly.

"Sidi, I—I—Sidi, I'm sorry! I did not mean—" stammered Aly, terrified at the way he had behaved.

The Caid reached for his turban, and began to knock off the loose sand.

"You were right, Aly. Praise be to Allah that you stopped me in time! I would have committed a grave sin. Okba does not deserve to die. He comes from a place where there are no snakes. It was my pride that made me behave like that. I was angered by the fall. It is the first time I have fallen from a horse since I was a stripling. Forgive me, Aly!"

"I—I—Sidi—!" was all the boy could gasp. "I know you would not hurt Okba."

"But for you I would have killed him! You saved his life, so now his life is yours. I give him to you, Aly ben Rabah. I am not fit to own such a horse. He is yours."

"But—But—" There was a roaring in Aly's ears. The dazzling sunshine seemed tinged with red as the blood pounded in his head. "You do not mean it, Sidi! I cannot own a horse. Okba is the most wonderful horse in the world, but he is for Caids and Emirs, not for a boy who works in a *fondouk*. I could not even feed him, Sidi."

The Caid had replaced his turban, and was smiling. His usual good temper had returned. He reached forward and stroked the stallion's silky nose.

"He is yours," he repeated. "He can continue to live

and eat in my stables, but he is wholly yours. You need no longer work in the *fondouk*. You can work for me. There are many things that you can do for me, and you can ride Okba at the same time."

"Sidi—!" Aly's voice was husky and he could barely whisper. "If you mean that—I will work my fingers to the bone. I will clean out your stables, groom your horses, water them, and—"

"I have stable boys for that," declared the Caid. "I shall have other things for you to do. You and Okba can serve me well. Now—up with you—and ride him back to the stables and tell them to saddle Manouba. I will wait here until you bring him back, then we will ride together to the camp of M'Loudi, where I have business."

Before Aly quite knew what was happening, he had been hoisted to the saddle. The stirrups were too long for him, and he was dizzy with an almost unbearable excitement, but he would not fall off, no matter how Okba behaved, for he realized that Ramdan ben Mizan actually meant what he said!

He was the owner of the finest horse in North Africa.

2 The Boy who was Envied

It was a month later, and Aly checked his horse at the corner where the Street of the Olive Trees ran into the Square of the Camels. His dog Fellah stopped beside him.

It was market day in Yelten, and the space before him was packed with people who had come from the surrounding desert. A seething mass of white-robed figures swarmed about the stalls and the shops in the colonnade which ran along three sides of the square. On the fourth side stood the mosque, a landmark for many miles around.

From his lofty seat on the white stallion Aly looked over the heads of the crowd. It was not easy to control a feeling of superiority, but he told himself that he was still the same Aly who a few weeks earlier had cleaned out stables.

His mother, his sister, and his crippled elder brother still lived in the mud house where he had been born. His best friends were still Selim the donkey boy, and Ibrahim, the blind water seller. He was the same sturdy, grave-faced boy whose ambition to own a horse had once seemed hopeless. Only his clothing had changed. Instead of a cotton robe he now wore tight white trousers to his ankles, and a short linen jacket. On his head was a turban interlaced with brown camel-hair cord, and on his feet were stout sandals, held in place by a single strap between his toes. He was well dressed.

A fakir was giving his performance to an appreciative

audience. Dodging about in the background, sometimes rising on tiptoe to try and see over those in front, was Aly's sister Mamounah. She was four years younger than he, and was not yet compelled to wear the veil. A plump, moon-faced little girl, always smiling, Aly was glad to see that she was wearing the new frock which he had bought her out of his first earnings.

He touched Okba lightly with his heel, and the stallion edged slowly forward, picking its way carefully through the moving throng.

"Ho, Aly!" called someone. "Greeting!"

Aly was about to reply when he saw his dog slinking off to a corner where some yellow hounds were lying in the sun. He knew that would mean a fight.

"Fellah!" he called, sharply. "Come back!"

Fellah was a saluki, tawny, with silky fringes to his tail and ears. He was as graceful as the gazelles which he was quite capable of running down, but he was also obedient. He turned back reluctantly and fell in behind Okba.

Mamounah had heard Aly's voice, and came running to him.

"I can't see the fakir," she complained breathlessly. "Let me sit up with you."

He reached down and caught her hand. She placed one bare foot on top of his in the wide stirrup, and the next moment had swung herself up in front of him, sitting sideways. With a happy gurgle she watched what the fakir was doing, for she could now see over the tallest of those in front.

The fakir, one of the sect called Aissaoua, was lean and gaunt, with a ragged robe which reached only to his knees, and long, black hair falling to his shoulders. He had been thrusting silver skewers into his face and tongue, apparently without inflicting harm, but now he was about to demonstrate a trick which never failed to thrill the onlookers.

His assistant was a boy of no more than ten years of age, thin and undersized, wearing only a loincloth. On the bare ground was a round, flat basket about a yard in diameter, perhaps fifteen inches in depth, with an opening at the top only large enough enough for a small boy to wriggle through.

The boy entered the basket, which he appeared to fill, and popped up his head to grin at the crowd before the fakir pushed it down with the basket-work lid, which completely closed the opening.

From a bundle of rags he now produced a long, thin sword, and made it flash in the sunlight, chanting in a high-pitched voice. The crowd was silent.

With a sudden hoarse cry the man plunged the sword through the basket from side to side, and a scream came from the boy inside. Mamounah shuddered enjoyably.

The fakir withdrew the sword, which was now stained red, and without a second's hesitation plunged it in again, from another angle, so that the point protruded on the other side. Once again he snatched it out, now dripping blood, and then seemed to go mad, jabbing, thrusting, and stabbing the basket from top and sides, from every possible angle.

The cries of the boy changed to groans, and finally there was silence. The fakir wiped his forehead, then cleaned the sword with the same rag. He snatched off the lid of the basket, and out jumped the grinning boy, quite unhurt, to take up a greasy tarboosh and carry it to the crowd for the collection.

Mamounah sighed, and was about to get Aly to explain once again how it was done, when the stallion gave an angry squeal and reared on its hind legs, scattering the people near it.

If Aly had not been quick in throwing an arm around his sister and clutching her to him, as he tightened his legs on the excited horse, both would have been hurled off.

As it was he fought for nearly a minute to subdue Okba, while men shouted, cursed, or offered advice. A circle had rapidly formed around them, everyone keeping their distance, and when Okba turned, blood-red nostrils flaring with anger, Aly saw on the ground the cause of the trouble, a thick leaf of the prickly pear, with many wicked, projecting spikes.

Someone was moving off through the crowd at the back, and looked around to grin. It was Musa, a tall, burly youth two years Aly's senior. He was the village bully, and hated Aly because he always defied him and was unafraid of him.

Aly's lean face grew stern, and his hands tightened on the reins. But for the surrounding crowd he would have urged Okba after the culprit, for he knew that Musa had thrown that prickly leaf at the horse. Musa had thought it funny, had hoped that Aly would be thrown, and that Okba would bolt through the market place.

Mamounah might have been thrown to the ground and trampled thought Aly, but aloud he comforted the girl and told her not to be alarmed.

Some of the bystanders, who were jealous of his recent good fortune, now began to rail at him for bringing such a dangerous horse into the crowd, but there were others who had seen the reason for Okba's panic, and shouted them down.

"I'll take you home. Sit still!" murmured Aly, and promised himself that before long he would make Musa pay for this spiteful trick.

They left the noise of the market behind them, and trotted between the high mud walls of the palm groves and orchards, where vegetables grew between the trees. These gardens were irrigated from deep wells. This was the only way in which the desert could be made to support life.

Aly's home was at the edge of the oasis, overlooking the

wadi which formed the southern boundary of Yelten. Beyond was the limitless desert.

Their humble mud-built house was in a small garden which provided them with much of their food. Yusuf, their brother, greeted them as they halted at the gateway. He was twenty years of age, crippled since birth, with one leg shorter than the other. Formerly he had been an ordinary camel driver, but thanks to Aly's influence he had now been made the Caid's head camel man. The money Aly earned had brought greater comfort to the family, and they ate meat or chicken at least once a week.

"You are just in time," called out Yusuf. "Our mother has made a rich stew with the remains of yesterday's chicken. You will eat with us, Aly?"

Mamounah had slipped to the ground, and Aly joined her, hitching the reins to a spike at the side of the gate.

"I cannot stay, Yusuf," he said. "The Caid is expecting me before noon, and I will be late. I will run in and see Salimah, then be on my way."

Salimah, their mother, was old and feeble, but very proud to think her sons were doing so well. She also pressed Aly to stay and eat with them, but understood when he explained that he had to report to the Caid about some missing sheep.

Leaving them to their meal, he called Fellah and rode through the oasis towards the big, white house where the Caid lived. It was there he stabled Okba.

The guards at the gateway nodded to him as he passed through. He was an accepted part of the household, although he returned home each night.

He went directly to the stable, a big, airy building which at times housed more than thirty horses, many of them pure Arab, although none had the appearance, speed, or stamina of Okba.

When the stallion was safely stabled and munching some oats, Aly found the Caid sitting in the inner courtyard. He had been listening to complaints by various persons, for it was he who dispensed the law in all local and domestic matters.

When Aly had greeted him according to custom, the Caid demanded: "Well, my son, what of Ali Said's missing sheep? Were they truly stolen?"

"No, Sidi. It seems that the shepherd was careless, and fifty of them strayed from the flock and became marooned on a rocky pinnacle. They were found before they could die of thirst."

"Allah be praised!" muttered the Caid. "Then there will be no need to hunt the thieves. What other news is there from the camp of Ali Said?"

Aly repeated all the gossip that he had heard during his morning visit to a nomad camp some eight miles to the south. The Caid was finding him extremely useful for getting first-hand information about his scattered people. He knew that the boy loved nothing better than a chance to make a journey on horseback, and sometimes he could pick up news which an older man might not hear.

At last the Caid nodded, and said: "Go and eat while there is still something left in the kichen. Your ride will have sharpened your appetite."

Aly was not sorry to be told this, for he was very hungry, but his lips tightened when he saw another boy about his own age hastening towards the kitchen from the stables. It was Sami, one of the stable-boys, and Aly had not seen him when he had stabled Okba. He wondered why Sami had kept out of his sight, but he was a secretive youth with a ferrety face. Unfortunately he was the son of the cook, and it was best to keep on the right side of him if one wanted good food.

The kitchen had no window, and was full of wood-smoke and savoury smells.

"Peace unto you, Sidi!" greeted Sami, in the doorway,

and Aly knew that the cook's son was mocking him because he was jealous of the position that he enjoyed with the Caid.

He kept his temper, and replied briefly: "And to you peace!" He went on: "I did not see you in the stable when I brought in Okba."

"I was not there," said Sami, his eyes widening, and before Aly could say that he had just seen him leaving the building, the boy had dodged behind his father and was presenting a plate to be piled with baked meats. Although very thin, Sami had an enormous appetite.

Aly got a bowl of meat stew and some corn pancakes. He retired to a table in a far corner, and wondered how he could save some of the meat for his friend, Selim, who never got enough to eat. Selim was an orphan, and earned a slender living by hiring out his donkey and himself for various tasks.

Aly solved the problem by making a gigantic sandwich of several pieces of meat between two of the pancakes. looking up, he saw Sami eyeing him balefully, and felt that the other's jealousy was turning to hatred.

But he did not worry that Sami had seen him make the big sandwich. The Caid would not grudge a little food going to one of Aly's friends.

He finished off his meal with a handful of dates, by which time Sami had disappeared. Aly carried the sandwich outside, and looked through the gateway to see if Selim was about. The stable-boy was not to be seen, but suddenly from the stable there came an angry squeal, and Aly recognized the cry of Okba. Something had hurt or scared the stallion.

He ran his hardest and burst into the stables a few moments later. Okba was rearing and plunging, only held by his headstall. As he strained back and flung himself from side to side, he was in grave danger of injuring himself on the baked mud walls.

"Okba!" cried Aly, dodging the flailing hoofs and slipping in beside the excited horse. "What is the matter? Gently! Gently!"

The stallion squealed again, and tugged back so violently that the rope which held him nearly broke. His eyes were bulging, and saliva dropped from his gaping mouth. His satiny skin was wet with sweat. He was in a rare panic.

Then Aly saw a movement among the oats in the trough from which Okba had been eating. At first he thought it was a rat, but when he had snatched up a stick to kill it, he saw a snake among the grain.

He quickly hooked it out with the stick, and stamped on its head, for it was small and comparatively harmless, a type which lived in the oasis gardens. Only when Aly had flicked the still writhing body out into the yard did Okba begin to quieten down, but it took much petting and soothing before he calmed completely. Even then he would not eat from the trough.

Aly had been doing some hard thinking.

Never before had he seen one of these snakes in the stables. They never entered buildings. He was certain that it had not been in the trough when he had poured in the oats. Furthermore, the trough was considerably clear of the ground, and snakes could not climb.

He looked up to see if the snake could have dropped from the roof, but that was of sun-baked tiles, and there were no openings. There could be only one explanation. The snake had been thrown into the oats by someone who wished to panic Okba, knowing his weakness.

"Sami!" decided Aly, remembering how the stable-boy had slipped out of the kitchen before him, and had denied being in the stable previously.

He looked around for Sami, but there was no sign of him. He would have found something to do in another part of the establishment, and would swear to his innocence. It would be impossible to prove that he had caught the snake and brought it to the stables, but there was enough evidence that he had done so.

Jealousy was a terrible thing, and it was not the first time Aly had encountered it since the Caid had seen fit to take him into his household.

It was the second time in one day that spite had been shown to Aly, and he felt miserable about it.

3 The Sandstorm

Aly rode fast over the desert, with Fellah not far behind. It was the morning following the incident in the market place, and he was on another errand for the Caid.

Word had come that a caravan of forty camels, bringing dates from the south, would pass within ten miles of Yelten on its way to the market in Biskra. That year the date harvest had been a failure in Yelten, and the Caid was anxious to purchase those forty loads of dates for his people. He had sent Aly to intercept the caravan and to ask the merchants to head for the oasis, something which the camel drovers should be glad to do, for it would save them several days.

It was early morning, with the eastern sky still richly glowing. The air was fresh, and Okba wanted to gallop, but Aly held him in check, as the going was rough and stony. It would be time enough to gallop when they came to the big, dried-up lake which lay across their path. There the surface would be smooth and friable.

He thrilled to the feel of the magnificent horse. Never in his wildest dreams had he hoped to own such a mount. He knew he would be forever grateful to Sidi Ramdan ben Mizan, and hoped that he would be able to accomplish his mission.

Away to the south a small group of gazelle sighted him, and fled over the dunes in a series of amazing leaps. Fellah raised his head and whined softly as he loped along. He wanted to give chase, but his master kept straight on.

"Not today, Fellah. We are on the Caid's business, and must not waste time."

The saluki was disappointed, but a few minutes later a slinking shape emerged from a hollow and raced ahead of them. Fellah was off in pursuit like an arrow from a bow. Aly did not check him, for it was a jackal, and he knew the dog would only chase it long enough to give it a scare. Fellah would not come to grips with the unclean scavenger.

Overhead a buzzard swooped hopefully. It had spotted the chase, and wondered if there would be a kill.

The loose stones clattered and scattered under Okba's flint-hard hoofs. It was an ugly stretch of country, and Aly was glad when they came to a shallow wadi, for beyond it there were wide strips of firm sand between the stones, and he could pick an easier path.

Fellah caught up as they climbed the farther side of the wadi, his tongue lolling, his brown eyes glistening with excitement.

"Foolish one," scolded Aly, "why do you tire yourself? We have far to go."

But he knew that however far they went, Fellah would be able to keep up.

They reached the *chott*, a dried-up lake with its salt-encrusted bed stretching as flat as a billiard table for three miles. There were many of these in North Africa, and they formed natural race tracks. Okba did not need a slight shake of the reins to encourage him to stretch at full gallop. He enjoyed a gallop as much as his young rider. Fellah wisely did not try to race with them; he knew he could overtake them on the other side.

The air sang past Aly's ears, and whipped the folds of the turban away from his face. His short jacket was un-buttoned and streamed out behind him like a cloak. He wanted to shout for the sheer joy of living. How much better this was than cleaning out the filth in the *fondouk*!

All too quickly they came to the other side. Okba's nostrils were distended, and he was blowing noisily, but his breathing was regular and unaffected. With that great depth of chest he could drink in air enough to supply all the oxygen he needed. Truly did the Arabs call these blood-horses: "Drinkers of the Wind".

They picked their way at a walk between clumps of spiky grey-green shrubs on which camels could graze with apparent enjoyment. It was strange how these bushes found sufficient moisture to exist in such places. They looked dried-up and almost dead, but there was still some sap in them.

There were other bushes in the desert which attracted moisture from the air by secreting salt on their leaves, but most of them relied on deep-probing roots which searched far below the surface for water. Nearly everywhere in the Sahara there was water if one could probe deeply enough.

Aly had heard that two hundred miles to the south-east of Yelten oil had been found, and that it was being piped from there to the Mediterranean coast. He was thinking about this, and wondering if he would ever see the sea, when he topped a sand dune and saw a moving cloud of dust in the distance.

It was on the track which ran northwards to Biskra, the track along which the date caravan would be trudging at a steady two miles an hour. But this dust cloud was being raised by something which moved much more swiftly. It would be a car or a heavy lorry, lurching and rocking over the rutted trail at a speed which left camels far behind.

Motor traffic was rapidly replacing camels over the main routes of the Sahara, but the four-legged "ships of the desert" were still the only form of transport possible over vast areas where no mechanical vehicle could penetrate. For things which did not need high-speed delivery, such as grain, dates, and charcoal, camels were still by far the cheapest form of transport.

The stallion's ears had pricked forward as he watched the distant dust cloud. Okba had seen few motor vehicles, and was still scared of them. Neither did he like camels, perhaps because of their smell. He would not drink with them from the same stream or trough.

As they neared the track where the dust had now settled, Aly looked north and south for some sign of the camels. He could see nothing moving. By now the sun had climbed high overhead and beat down with savage intensity. The sand reflected the glare, and made him half close his eyes.

"Did Kassim pass last night, or has he not yet come?" he thought, Kassim being the leader of the caravan. "They should be in sight by now."

He rode onto the track, and dismounted. Forty camels could not have passed without leaving traces. He wandered for fifty yards on either side of the track, and assured himself that the caravan had not yet gone by.

He frowned as he strained his eyes to the south. Something must have delayed it, for the information they had received in Yelten was that it would be passing this point that morning.

It was an anti-climax to his ride. He had expected before now to have ridden up importantly to Kassim and given him the Caid's message, then to hasten back to Yelten to tell the Caid that the dates were on the way. Now he must either wait until the camels came in sight or ride south to meet them. The desert to the south was so flat that he should be seeing their dust if they were within five or six miles. He did not relish riding farther than that under the blistering sun.

There was no shade, no rocks, and no vegetation. The

trampled sand stretched endlessly on either side. A sound in the brassy sky made him look up. An airplane was passing, heading south.

Okba stamped impatiently. Fellah lay down and panted. Aly unslung from the saddle the goat skin water bag which he had brought with him. The horse and the dog looked at him expectantly.

He drank sparsely, for it was not wise to drink deeply in that heat. With him he had a battered tin can, and this he filled with water, once for Fellah, and once to hold to Okba's nose to let him clear the dust from his throat. With a damp rag he wiped the sand from the stallion's nostrils. Few Arabs would have done as much for their mount, but few owned such a superb animal.

It was as he remounted that he noticed a small puff of dust to the south. It was not the expected caravan, for it was moving too fast; it was not a motor vehicle, for it was moving too slowly. He shaded his eyes, and decided that it was a solitary horseman.

After a few moments of hesitation he rode to meet the man, hoping that he might have news of Kassim.

Twenty minutes later they were near enough to exchange shouts. The lone rider was from the camel train, and he had bad news.

The camels had stopped for the previous night in open country some five miles east of the track for Biskra. An hour before dawn the camp had been swept by bullets, which had killed two of the men, wounded three others, and stampeded the camels. The attackers had fired from behind the dunes.

"But who were they?" demanded Aly, on hearing this. "Touaregs?"

He was remembering stories he had heard of the Veiled Ones who had preyed on caravans earlier in the century.

"No," panted the man, who was almost as exhausted as his horse. "They were French, and they were in uniform.

There were seven or eight, and some of them had guns that spoke many times."

He imitated the sound of a Sten gun.

Aly was appalled.

"French soldiers! But why did French soldiers do this? Did they mistake you for rebels?"

"I do not know. When we ran and hid they entered the camp and took food and water. Then they rode away to the north-west on our best camels. Kassim and the others are trying to round up the rest of the camels, but with so many men dead and wounded it will be many hours before they are able to move. Kassim has ordered me to ride to Biskra and tell the Commandant there what has happened. Perhaps he will send airplanes to catch these men."

Aly was no longer paying attention to what was being said. He was considering something the man had mentioned earlier.

"You say that when they left you they rode to the north-west—in the direction of Yelten?"

"Yes, they took our best camels, and if they keep going long enough they will come to Yelten," agreed the other. "My horse is tired, and will not take me to Biskra. Lend me yours that I may reach there in good time."

Aly backed away in dismay. The idea of handing over Okba to a stranger was intolerable, even in such an emergency. Besides, he had other cause for alarm.

If these madmen came to Yelten without warning, they could cause great trouble. By then they would be in need of fresh mounts and further supplies, and they might kill to secure these. The Caid must be warned. Aly's own family must be protected.

"No, I must hasten back to tell my people that danger is on the way," he protested, suddenly putting foot to a stirrup and swinging to the stallion's back. "Keep going along the track and you are bound to meet someone who will take your message to Biskra."

He kicked in his heels and went away at a gallop, Fellah bounding after them. The man shouted angrily, but Aly was already disappearing in a cloud of dust, and there was nothing he could do but follow the boy's suggestion.

Aly slowed up before he had covered a mile. They had ten miles to go, and he must conserve Okba's strength.

He was greatly perturbed by the news, and tried to recollect what the country was like through which the soldiers would have to pass. They would have to cover about twenty miles to his ten, and his recollection was that it was mostly dune country, heavy going even for the strongest of camels. They had left Kassim's camp at dawn, so they had several hours' start on him.

It was imperative that he get word to the Caid as soon as possible. He maintained a steady canter, and presently noticed that the sky to the south was darkening. A hot wind was coming from the same direction.

"*Cheheli!*" he muttered in alarm, and tasted sand upon his lips.

The *cheheli*, known further north as the sirocco, was a hot wind which blew from the south at that time of the year and carried sand as far as the Mediterranean. It brought sandstorms which sometimes lasted three days. Travellers in the desert were terrified of this wind, and tried to reach shelter before the waves of sand overtook them.

Speed was more necessary than ever, but by now they had reached a region of flat, broken rock which lay like scattered flagstones over a wide area. Aly was compelled to drop Okba to a walk. To attempt to go faster would mean risking the stallion's legs.

Okba scented the oncoming sandstorm, and did his best, stepping out as rapidly as feasible, but it was soon evident that the clouds of sand from the south were gaining on them.

The light was becoming dim. Great clouds of sand almost blotted out the sun, which had shrunk to a small red ball at which one could look without discomfort to the eyes.

Sand and grit whipped his face and made Okba turn his head to the left. Fellah moved at a crouching run, his tail down, his tongue sand-coated as it hung from his panting jaws.

The wind was increasing in force, and now it had turned cold, chilling Aly through his thin clothing as it lashed him with particles of sharp sand. He covered his mouth and nose with the folds of his turban, and breathed through this to filter out some of the dust.

Okba snorted and blew as his nostrils became clogged, and wanted to swing to the north in order to have the wind behind him. Aly had to fight to hold the horse's head to the east.

Then he remembered that it would be just as bad for the soldiers.

The thought cheered him, and when they suddenly came to the edge of the *chott*, with its three-mile stretch of smooth, unbroken surface, his spirits rose.

"Let's go!" he shouted to Okba, letting the stallion have its head.

The horse leaped forward, and even the painful lashing of the sand in his face did not dismay Aly. He shut his eyes, and kept his head down, hoping that Fellah would be able to keep up.

The storm was now at its worst. The air seemed solid with dust and grit. It was increasingly difficult to breathe. Once the stallion faltered, almost stopped, and had a coughing fit, but after a few moments it continued the mad gallop.

They could see only a few yards ahead, but Aly knew there were no obstacles. He must judge by time alone when they were nearing the other side, for there was a

thirty-foot cliff which had to be climbed before they could continue their way to Yelten.

Then Okba splayed his legs and slithered to a stop so suddenly that Aly was thrown forward on the horse's neck. They had reached the farther side of the *chott* sooner than he had expected, and had only just avoided running headlong into the cliff.

"Bravo, Okba!" he muttered, and patted the sweat-blackened neck before him. "Now we have not far to go."

Confidently he sought the way to the top, but he could not find it. The cliff was almost sheer, and in places it overhung. They had changed direction while crossing the open *chott*, and had turned too far to the north, or too far to the south. It was impossible to tell which.

Partially sheltered from the driving sand by the cliff, they moved a hundred yards to the right before finding a place where it was possible to climb.

Okba's powerful quarters drove them to the top in a series of scrambling jumps, and there they met the full force of the sand-laden wind straight in their faces. Choking and gasping, Aly allowed the horse to swing to the left. They had been going due south instead of south-west. It was impossible to get their bearings when all landmarks were hidden.

Something white loomed up in the yellow haze, and he glimpsed a few stunted palms and a domed roof.

He remembered that on the south side of the *chott* there was an abandoned tomb which had been the home of a marabout, or holy man. This was it, half buried in the sand.

"We are miles out of our way!" he thought, despairingly. 'Okba must have turned south after stopping to cough. Perhaps we can shelter there until the worst is past."

He dismounted, and tugged the horse forward by the reins, then, remembering his dog, turned to call in a cracked voice: "Fellah! Fellah!"

4 Aly's Desperate Choice

The entrance to the tomb was almost silted up with driven sand. It was impossible to get Okba inside.

Aly led the horse to the leeward side and tethered it to a palm tree. Okba at once turned his tail to the wind, and sank his head in dejected resignation. Aly unhitched the waterskin.

"I will bring you a drink," he muttered, and returned to the tomb.

The chamber was circular, and no more than fourteen feet across, but it gave some shelter from the sand-blast outside. It would be wise to stay there until the storm eased up, and he could get his bearings.

Having shaken the loose sand from the folds of his turban, and wiped some of it from his face, he swallowed a few mouthfuls of water, then remembered his promise to Okba. He wished he could have brought the horse under cover.

Something darkened the small entrance for a moment, and slid down beside him. It was Fellah, whining with misery, but when he had lapped up some water he settled down stoically.

"Let us hope it will not last for long," murmured Aly, as he fondled the dog's silky ears. "Those madmen will not be able to get through to Yelten while the sand blows."

He went to Okba and gave him half the remaining

water. The stallion could have drunk three times as much.

"We must be patient," Aly told him. "In Allah's good time the wind will stop, and we will be on our way."

As there was nothing else to do, he returned to the chamber, lay down on the sandy floor, and slept with his head pillowed on Fellah.

He was awakened by the growling of the saluki. How long he had slept he could not tell, but it seemed a little clearer outside.

Fellah, staring towards the entrance, growled again. Aly got to his feet. It was then that he heard voices and the bellowing of camels.

He scrambled up the sloping mound of sand and crawled outside. The wind was dropping, and the air was clearing. Two dim, white figures were standing beside Okba, talking excitedly. The light was not good enough to show them clearly, but one was of immense size.

"Ho, there!" called Aly. "Peace be with you!"

They swung around as he came towards them, and he saw that they were not Arabs. They were white from the dust which coated them from head to foot.

The shorter of the pair, powerful and thickset, snarled something in a language which Aly did not understand, and jerked up his hand. The boy found himself looking into the barrel of a heavy revolver. At the same time the other man swung something from his back and held it at hip level. It was a Sten gun.

In the background other men were forcing the camels to their knees, but Aly was only vaguely aware of this, for the man with the revolver now said in Arabic with a harsh accent: "Come here!"

Trembling, Aly approached until the gun was almost touching him. He saw that these men wore uniforms with baggy trousers and ankle-length boots. They had *kepis* on their heads, the headgear worn by the soldiers of the Foreign Legion.

These were the men who had shot up Kassim's camp. Those camels were stolen. These were the men whom he had feared would reach Yelten before him. Like himself, they had lost their way in the sandstorm, and had turned too far to the north. By chance they had stumbled upon the palm trees and the marabout's tomb.

"How many are with you?" demanded the man, his small vicious eyes peering out of a mask of sand and sweat.

He spoke Arabic like one accustomed to it, but with a guttural accent.

Aly tried to reply, but his mouth was dry.

"I am alone, Sidi!" he managed to gasp at last. "I was sheltering from the storm."

His interrogator was a sergeant, a man of about forty, with blond hair and bushy eyebrows. Aly guessed him to be a German. He had seen many Germans in the detachments of the Foreign Legion which had from time to time passed through the district.

"Whose horse is this?" demanded the sergeant.

"It is mine, Sidi."

"You lie!" He swung his hand to Aly's head so viciously that the boy fell to the ground. "You lie! None such as you would own such a horse."

There was a sudden growl, and something launched itself at the sergeant's throat. It was Fellah, who until then had remained quietly behind his master.

The dog's weight threw the sergeant back against the man behind him. By then Fellah had hold of his gun arm. Either accidentally, or purposely, the German pulled the trigger, and the shot buried itself in the sand.

Then the bigger man lashed out with his foot, catching Fellah in the stomach, lifting him into the air to fall against a tree a dozen feet away, where he lay in a huddled heap.

"Fellah!" cried Aly, forgetting his own hurt, and trying to scramble up.

A huge hand closed on his neck and lifted him so that his feet were clear of the ground. He found himself gazing into the expressionless face of the sergeant's companion, a face in which the only noticeable features were a broken nose and wide, staring, blue eyes.

"Put him down, Polskie!" ordered the sergeant, ramming the revolver into Aly's stomach. "Now then, tell the truth! Where is the owner of that horse? How many are inside there?"

A half-dozen men had run forward at sound of the shot. They glared towards the small, domed building. They were all heavily armed. Unshaven, some bearded, with bloodshot eyes and hard, ruthless expressions, they had something of the appearance of desperate animals.

Aly gulped, and tried not to look towards his dog.

"Sidi, I told you the truth! The horse is mine. I am in the service of the Caid of Yelten, and was on an errand for him when the storm overtook me. There is nobody with me."

He thought it wiser not to mention that he had already encountered someone who had told him about the attack on Kassim's caravan.

The sergeant rapped out something in German. Three of the men ran over to the tomb. One fired a long burst from his gun through the opening, and the bullets could be heard ricocheting around the walls inside.

After a few moments one went inside and called out that the place was empty. The sergeant lowered his gun, and relaxed. Aly wanted to go to Fellah, but dared not move. He wondered how long it would be before they killed him.

There was something strange about these soldiers of the Legion. They all appeared to be German, except the ox-like man who was called Polskie, and whom the others treated with contempt.

It was not unusual to find Germans in the French Foreign Legion. They outnumbered all the other races, and most of the non-commissioned officers were German, but even though the Legionaries were notorious for their toughness and for the ruthless way they treated the Arabs, they did not go around murdering and robbing as these had done.

There was no officer with them. The sergeant was in charge. Aly began to think they were deserters. Even in Yelten they had heard there had been serious trouble in the Legion recently.

A push, a kick, sent him stumbling towards the tomb.

"Inside!" snapped the sergeant.

He bellowed something to the others, then followed Aly inside. Behind them came Polskie, bringing a water-skin and a sack. Aly was pushed down against the rear wall, where he crouched miserably, wondering why he had not been killed.

The sergeant grabbed the waterskin and took a long drink, after which he barked at his companion, who nodded agreement.

Aly knew no German, so could not follow what they said, but presently the sergeant turned to him and demanded in Arabic: "This Yelten— How far is it from here?"

"About five kilometres, Sidi."

"Which direction?"

"I do not know, Sidi. I was lost in the sandstorm, but when it clears I will get my bearings."

The sergeant considered, then asked, "How many people in Yelten? Any French soldiers?"

Aly told him what he wanted to know, and he nodded grimly before sending Polskie outside with a message for the others. Three of them returned with the big man, and squatted around, almost filling the chamber. The sergeant opened the sack and distributed some of the food which they had stolen from Kassim's camp. There were stale corn pancakes, a hunk of meat, some cheese made from camel's milk, and dates. They ate ravenously, and washed it down with water. Not once did they glance at Aly or offer him anything.

He only ventured to speak once: "My dog, Sidi—? Fellah—?"

"It's dead," was the callous reply. "Or if it isn't, it ought to be!"

Aly swallowed hard. He did not think the saluki would die so easily, but he hated to think of it lying there, perhaps badly injured.

Those outside must have had their own rations, for they did not come in to share with the others. They were guarding the camels, and watching that they were not taken by surprise.

The sand still drifted by in clouds, but it was not as thick as formerly. In a few hours visibility would have greatly improved.

When everyone had eaten, the sergeant took the waterskin and the remaining rations to one side of the chamber and lay down to sleep. The others followed his example, with the exception of Polskie, who was ordered to keep awake. He sat to one side of the entrance, a gun across his knees.

Time passed. Aly tried to figure out what he could do. He could not understand why they had not killed him. Of what use could he be to them? By nightfall the sandstorm would have died down, and they would be able to move off. Did they intend taking him with them?

He remembered Okba tethered under the palms. These men had arrived on camels, but when they left it was certain that the sergeant would ride the stallion. Aly could think of no way of preventing this.

The Pole looked stupid and sleepy, but it would be impossible to slip past him. Once when Aly changed his position to ease his cramped legs, the man growled angrily, and swung the gun to point at him.

The others snored and muttered in their sleep. They were on the verge of exhaustion.

The afternoon passed, and darkness had come, when someone shouted in at the entrance. The sergeant stirred, yawned, and sat up. He shouted questions, and got replies. He rose and kicked the others awake. They all crawled outside.

When the sergeant drew his revolver Aly thought his last moment had come, but the man only looked to see that it was fully loaded, and gestured towards the entrance.

"Outside, and remember that I'm behind you!"

Aly obeyed, finding that the wind had died away and the air was now clear. It was possible to see the stars overhead.

His first thought was for Fellah, but when he looked towards the spot where the dog had been lying, it was no longer there. Had Fellah recovered, and crawled away? He dared not ask, but his hopes rose.

The men were gathered around the camels, and seemed to be waiting for the sergeant to decide something.

Sergeant Franz Hummel, for that was his name, gripped Aly by the elbow and marched him to the edge of the clump of wizened palms.

"Where is Yelten?" he demanded.

Aly stared across the desert, and his eyes turned half-left. Far away was a ridge which he thought he recognized. A few kilometres beyond that was the oasis which formed his little world, but instinct warned him against blurting this out. He pretended to be doubtful, turning this way and that.

"Hurry!" growled Hummel, nudging him with the gun. "Yelten—which way? Either you show us the way—or—"

He left his threat unfinished. Aly's heart pounded. These men were going to Yelten. They wanted him to guide them. The manner in which they had treated Kassim and his party was an indication of how they would behave in the oasis. Although they were only eight in number, they were heavily armed, and the Caid's men would stand no chance against them. Outlaws from their own people, they would want food, clothing, horses, perhaps money. They would strip the oasis of everything of value before they went away, and if there was any resistance they would kill without mercy.

"Well—?" thundered the leader of the deserters. "Don't you know the way to your own home?"

Aly's brain was working fast. He suddenly knew what he must do. Five miles to the south of Yelten there was another oasis, part of the Caid's territory. Once it had been a flourishing palmery, with three wells, supporting several hundred people, but as so often happened in the Sahara, the underground streams had changed direction, and the wells had begun to run dry.

There had been insufficient water to irrigate the crops. Even the long roots of the palms had failed to find the moisture they needed to keep them alive. They had withered and died. The inhabitants had withdrawn to Yelten. Now they only went there when they needed wood for fuel.

Some sickly palms still fought feebly against the encroaching sand, and there were enough of them to form a dark patch in the starlight, but many of them were dead where they stood, and none of them produced fruit. This place of death was called Ain Zara.

These men could do no harm there. Aly had made his desperate choice.

He raised his arm and pointed to the south-east.

"There is Yelten, Sidi!" he said firmly, and hoped they would not notice that he was shaking. "Only five or six kilometres from here."

"Good!" grunted the sergeant. "We are going there, and you are coming with us. If by chance you have made a mistake, I shall shoot you through the legs and leave you in the desert to die."

Aly licked dry lips as he was led back to the tethered Okba. Someone had given the stallion water. It stretched its neck towards Aly, and whinnied. He would have gone forward, but Hummel caught him by the shoulder and pulled him back.

"Not so fast!" he rasped. "What do you call him?"

"Okba!"

"Okba, eh? Let us hope he lives up to his name, and carries me to victory!"

"But Sidi—!" pleaded Aly, desperately. "He will let no one but me ride him."

"Is that so?" The sergeant approached the restive horse, which rolled wary eyes. "Then you shall ride him, and I will ride behind you. Mount!"

Any hope Aly may have had of making a dash for freedom faded when two of the others grabbed and held the stallion's head as he swung to the saddle. Hardly had he settled when Hummel was up behind him, one arm around his waist, prodding his back with the revolver.

"Lead the way to Yelten!" commanded the sergeant. "Remember I've a gun. One false move—and you'll never make another."

Okba trembled at the feel of a stranger on his back. His arched neck was damp with sweat. Aly soothed him with soft words and gentle pats, and they moved slowly forward in the direction of Ain Zara. Behind them the rest of the party climbed onto their camels and forced them to their feet.

"Do not go fast because of the camels," growled the German. "You should be pleased that I am letting you ride home on your own horse! Many another would have shot you back there, and left your miserable carcass to rot."

Aly did not reply. Perhaps it would have been better if he had died back there. His fate would be even less pleasant when they discovered that he had tricked them, but he would have gained time for those in Yelten. Not even to save his own life would he lead these human wolves to his friends.

As the line of camels followed Okba, a slim, tawny shape came unseen from the shadows of the palms and followed at a safe distance.

Fellah limped badly, but he did not intend to let his young master out of sight.

5 The Dead Oasis

The desert was silvered by the starlight. There was no moon, but it was possible to see for miles. The air was now free from dust, and each star shone as though it had been burnished.

In the morning the dawn would be exceptionally beautiful. It was always so after a sandstorm.

The men with Ali were not thinking about such things. They talked about what they might find in Yelten, and about their ultimate escape from Algeria.

Serious trouble had come to the First Battalion of the Foreign Legion, to which these men had belonged. The battalion had been involved in a rising against the French Government. As a punishment it was going to be disbanded, and the men distributed among other loyal regiments. Some of the Germans stationed at Colomb Bechar, in eastern Algeria, had decided to desert rather than submit to this.

Sergeant Hummel had been a natural leader, and with six of his own countrymen, and a Pole named Wolny, had stolen a truck, loaded it with supplies and weapons, and fled.

Cunningly, they headed east into the waterless, trackless desert, rather than make directly for the coast. This had misled their pursuers, and they had got a hundred miles away before the truck had run out of fuel. After that they had been obliged to go on foot, loading much of their food and water on the broad back of the uncomplaining Wolny.

Wolny was feeble-minded, and answered to the name of Polskie. The sergeant had brought him along because of his tremendous strength.

When they had been almost at the end of their tether, they had come upon the camp of Kassim and had attacked it ruthlessly, taking camels and supplies. They had been seeking some lonely oasis, where they might rest and prepare for a dash to the Tunisian border, when the sandstorm had overtaken them and they had lost direction.

Now, with Aly's aid, they hoped to use Yelten as their base until they were ready to move on. They had learned from him that no troops were stationed there, and that there was no telegraphic communication with Biskra. They intended to force the inhabitants to give them shelter until the hue and cry had died down.

They did not know that the boy was leading them astray!

Despite vigorous beating, the camels could not move at more than three miles an hour. Okba was well ahead when a dark patch was seen in the starlight.

A grunt of satisfaction came from Hummel, who still had tight hold of Aly, although he had returned the revolver to its holster.

"Yelten?" he demanded.

"Yelten," repeated Aly.

From a distance it was impossible to see that the palms were dying, and that sand covered the former gardens. The sergeant turned and shouted the news to the others.

"Which is the best way into the village?" he next demanded.

"There is a pathway up the other side of the wadi," Aly told him, remembering that his last visit to the abandoned oasis had been with Selim and his donkey to fetch firewood.

"Lead the way, and if you give warning of our coming you know what to expect!"

Aly made no reply. They still had about two miles to go, and then he would have to face the consequences of his trickery.

Strangely, he was no longer afraid. He took courage from the feel of the horse beneath him. On foot he would have been terrified, but he felt a different person when astride Okba. On foot he would have been conscious that he was the son of a poor *fondouk* keeper. Mounted on the stallion, he was the emissary of the Caid, someone of consequence, someone who must show courage and initiative.

He no longer trembled with apprehension when they came to the wide, stony bed of the dried-up river which formed the northern boundary of Ain Zara. The banks were low. There was little climbing to be done, and the track was clearly visible.

Hummel made Aly halt until the camels had come up.

"We're not taking these brutes any further to risk them giving the alarm," he said. "They can be left here with Polskie, and you can follow on foot. Leave everything but your guns and ammunition."

"And you, sergeant—?" demanded someone.

"I stay on the horse. The boy will show the way to the Caid's house. Once we have the Caid prisoner we will hold him hostage for the good conduct of the rest, but until then move as quietly as possible. There are bound to be dogs, and they'll raise an uproar at the slightest sound."

Aly did not understand what was being said. He was wondering whether it would be possible to get rid of the sergeant when they were among the palms. It was his only chance. Once the deserters realized how they had been fooled, they would show him no mercy.

"Forward!" growled Hummel, and again prodded Aly

with his revolver. "Lead the way to the house of the Caid."

Aly walked Okba across the old river bed. He was glad there was no moon, or they might have discovered his deception sooner.

Behind Okba came the others, guns and automatic rifles at the ready. They were trained killers. They intended to shoot down anyone who opposed them.

The Pole remained with the camels.

Aly marvelled that the unnatural silence did not warn them that something was wrong. No sound came from the dark mass of palms ahead. The dry fronds did not rustle. Not even a jackal slunk out of the shadows.

They climbed the track on the other side. Glistening bones shone in the starlight under one of the shrivelled palms. A camel had died there when the last of the inhabitants had been leaving.

"A dreary-looking dump!" muttered someone.

"Shut up!" growled the sergeant, but he frowned at the sight of several gaunt stumps without leaves, and snarled in Aly's ear: "Why have the palms died?"

"The sand, Sidi!" muttered Aly, wishing his passenger would let go his waist for just one moment. It might be possible to make Okba rear suddenly.

The pathway made an abrupt turn, and proved to be completely blocked by a sand drift which rose to a height of six feet. Even the sergeant could tell that it had not been formed during the recent sandstorm. Immediately suspicious, he raised an open hand and rocked Aly with a blow across the ear.

"Fool—this is not the way!"

Before Aly could reply, there was a snarl from alongside, and Fellah bounded out of the shadows. His teeth closed on the sergeant's leg, piercing the tough uniform trousers.

He hung on, but it was not only his weight that proved Hummel's undoing. The sergeant let go his hold on Aly as he twisted to strike at the dog with his revolver, and at that moment Okba reared. Aly had jerked on the reins.

The German was thrown backwards over the horse's tail, and landed heavily on the ground, the barrel of his revolver being driven into the sand. Fellah sprang for his throat, and the two rolled over and over as the others ran forward to aid their leader.

Aly urged Okba at the barrier before them, and the stallion's hoofs barely touched the top as it cleared the obstacle.

"Fellah! Fellah!" shouted Aly, as he kicked in his heels.

Shouts, oaths, and shots sounded behind him, but the path twisted and turned before reaching the former village square, and none of the shots came near him.

He was in what had once been the centre of Ain Zara. On all sides were mud huts in a state of ruin, most without roofs, some with only two walls. All the timber had been removed when the place had been abandoned, and had been taken to Yelten. Mud bricks were easy to make, but wood was precious in the Sahara. Nothing of value had been left behind.

This was the dead place to which Aly had led the deserters, and thanks to Fellah he had escaped their vengeance. A loud panting told him that the dog had likewise escaped. It ranged alongside as he rode for the farther side of the village.

"Fellah, I feared you were dead!" he murmured, and the saluki looked up at him with lolling tongue.

Behind them the sergeant was urging his men in pursuit. They were shooting as they came, sweeping the silent village with their bullets. They had not yet realized that the place was uninhabited. They meant to overawe the villagers before they were properly awake.

Aly could have ridden straight out of the oasis and back to Yelten, but he did not choose to do so. He meant to further mislead the deserters.

He knew they had completely lost their bearings. Ain Zara was not marked on any map, even if they had one. They could not see Yelten from Ain Zara. When they came to leave the dead oasis, they must have no idea which way to go in order to reach Yelten.

To make sure of this he must give them a false clue. He must show himself riding in a different direction.

When he reached the edge of the oasis, he stopped and waited. Back in the deserted village there was fresh uproar. Hummel and his comrades had discovered how they had been fooled. Voices were rising, and loudest of these was the sergeant's. He was bellowing for them to calm down.

"The boy tricked us!" he growled. "But we're here, and we're tired. We've got enough food to go on with, and there's nobody to bother us. Tell Polskie to bring in the camels, and we'll get some sleep. When daylight comes we'll decide what to do."

It was common sense. The disgruntled men needed rest. The night was yet young. One of them went to help the Pole bring the camels across the wadi.

Aly waited until they had settled. In the meantime he unsaddled Okba and rubbed his back with sand. He found a few dry dates beneath one of the dying palms, and shared these with his two companions. He was thirsty, but he had no water. He knew the Germans had several full water-skins, and wondered if he could get one of these.

The camels had been brought in and unloaded. Hummel had posted a sentry, and the rest of the party were sleeping in one of the roofless houses. Aly decided that it was time to make a move.

He had given Okba's back a much needed rest. Now he saddled up again, but he did not mount. Instead, he led the stallion to the eastern side of the oasis, and left it in charge of Fellah, whom he ordered not to move.

He crept towards the village and the sleeping intruders.

It was not difficult to find out where the sentry was

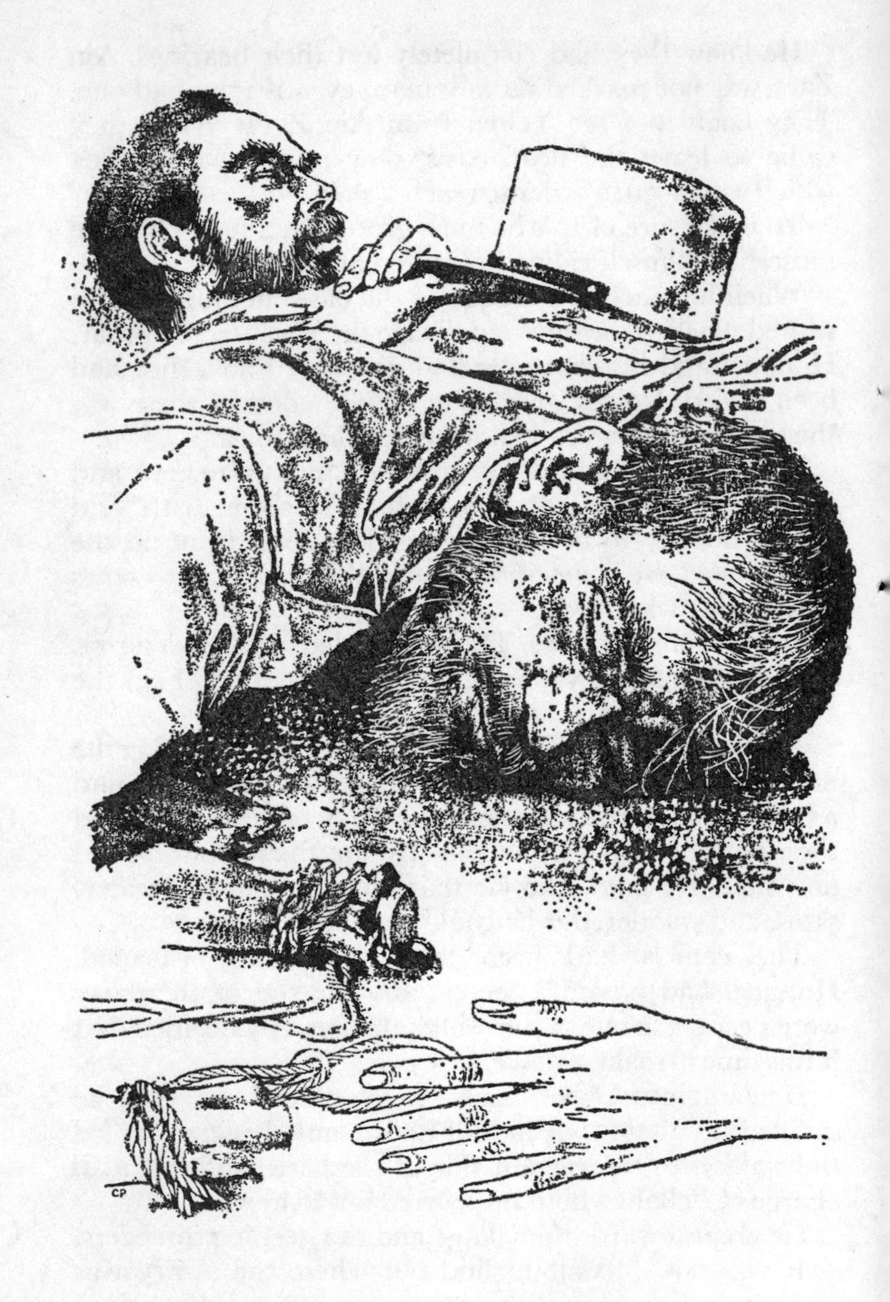

sitting close under a wall. The camels were barracked nearby, stolidly chewing as they stared into the darkness. They paid no attention to the crawling figure of Aly.

It was his intention to let himself be seen, but not before he had secured one of the waterskins. Inch by inch he crept towards the house from which the sound of snoring came. He was in no hurry. Sometimes he remained motionless for minutes at a time. Whenever the sentry glanced in his direction he froze in his tracks.

The man was sleepy. He kept nodding, and there came a time when his eyes closed. Aly reached the doorway, and peered inside.

As his eyes became accustomed to the gloom, he made out the sprawling figures. Two waterskins lay between the sergeant and the big Pole. The nearer was only half full. Aly lay flat and reached for it. He could touch it with the tips of his fingers. He eased forward another few inches, and got a grip on the rope that tied the narrow neck. He began to drag it as he backed away.

The sentry wakened, coughed, and crossed his legs the other way. He stared out under the palms, and did not glance behind him. Aly lay still until the man had settled down again, then continued to pull the waterskin out of the doorway. Finally he had it round the corner, and lifted it knee-high. Crouching, he made for the nearest palms.

He looked back. The sentry was still unaware that anything was happening. It was time to give him a rude awakening. Aly tilted the waterskin and squeezed it violently. There was a loud gurgling noise from the water inside, and the sentry came to his feet and stared.

Aly began to run, carrying the waterskin with him. He hoped he would be screened by the palms before the man could get the rifle to his shoulder.

Crack! A bullet thudded into one of the trees, and the sentry's shout brought the sleepers to their feet.

Aly made no secret of his going. He made as much noise as possible as he ran towards Okba. More bullets followed him, but in the shadow of the palms he was a difficult target, and he zig-zagged to make it harder still. Men were running after him. That was what he had hoped; he wanted them to see him ride away.

He reached the stallion well ahead of his pursuers, hoisted the waterskin before him on the high pommel of the saddle, and scrambled up. A touch of his heels, and Okba was away, Fellah close behind.

Shouts came from those who had reached the edge of the oasis. They opened fire. It was a moment of danger for Aly, but he was gambling on the poor light, his speed, and their excitement. A bullet tore the elbow of his thin jacket, but neither he, the horse, nor the dog was hit.

Minutes later he was out of range, and slowed to mock at the infuriated men who had come out from under the palms.

"Farewell!" he called. "I will see you in Yelten."

They poured bullets in his direction, but without result. He shook up Okba, who settled down to a steady canter, heading due east, into trackless country which he knew led to the terrible "sea of stones". Yelten was not in that direction, nor any other inhabited place, but Aly believed that when Hummel and the others saw him going that way they would believe he was making for Yelten.

His tracks would be marked in the sand as clearly as on a chart, but when he reached the stones, which showed no tracks, he would turn north, and cut across the dunes to the oasis.

"When daylight comes, they will follow my trail out here, and get themselves lost," he reasoned. "By that time I will be in Yelten, telling the Caid all about these men. He will send for help to Biskra."

He rode on until he was out of sight of Ain Zara, then

stopped to drink from the waterskin, and to share the remainder with Fellah and Okba.

They had a long way to go before dawn, but he was confident that he had averted the danger that had threatened Yelten.

6 The Alarm

The oasis was in sight, a dark green island on a sea of pink sand, for the sun was rising, and the whole of the desert was bathed in a rosy glow.

Aly was approaching from the east. Behind him, a dozen miles distant, the Aurès Mountains curved from the north. Mists hid the lower part of these rugged ranges, and the peaks appeared to be floating on cotton-wool.

Okba was showing no sign of fatigue, for Aly had held a steady pace, as much for the sake of the saluki as anything else. It had been hard going for Fellah, but he was not far behind, tail streaming out parallel with the ground, the silky fringes of his ears lifting like butterfly wings to each springy bound. Both dog and horse were desperate for a drink. The water in the goat skin was long since finished.

During the past hours one slinking jackal had been the only sign of life that Aly had encountered, but he knew that the first rays of sunlight would cause the people of Yelten to bestir themselves.

He descended by a gentle slope into the wadi, and rode along the old river bed to the waterhole below the village. Here the Yelten boys soon would be bringing their animals to drink, mostly donkeys and goats, but there would be a sprinkling of horses too.

Okba snorted and pulled as soon as he sighted the pool.

Aly checked him with difficulty, slid from the saddle, and slipped the bit from the stallion's mouth. Fellah had already waded in knee-deep, and was lapping greedily. The water was salty, but desert-bred animals were accustomed to that, and would have missed the saline tang if they had been given absolutely fresh water.

As the horse drank, Aly looked at the steep path which led to the village. Someone had arrived at the top with two goats. It was a girl, and he recognized her as Amira, a friend of his sister. She was the first at the wadi that morning.

The goats did not need driving to the water. They skipped down the pathway at breakneck speed, taking short cuts where the path twisted, leaving Amira far behind. She did not hurry herself, for she knew they would go no farther than the pool.

She greeted Aly gravely: "Peace be with you, Aly! Mamounah says that you were lost in the sandstorm."

"Yes, I had to take shelter," he told her, "but no harm was done. Now I go to the Caid."

He rode slowly up the pathway. Amira shouted something after him as he neared the top, but he did not catch the words, although he waved to show that he had heard.

He was desperately tired, but was kept going by the urgency of his news. But first he told Fellah to go home. If they saw the saluki his family would know he was back. Fellah left him reluctantly.

Aly took a pathway through the palm groves. It was very peaceful with the early sun slanting through the delicate fronds, and casting lace-like shadows on the ground. Everything glistened with dew, and he was glad to see it, for every spot of water squeezed from the atmosphere was valuable.

Beneath the palms they grew grain and vegetables. Narrow channels carried the water, which was let into each cultivated patch from the irrigation ditches at certain hours of the day. It was a highly organized system, the water being drawn up from deep wells by donkeys or horses which circled endlessly at the end of long, wooden shafts.

This irrigation system had been developed through the centuries, and if it failed, life itself would fail.

There were fruit trees as well as date-bearing palms, oranges, lemons, figs, apricots, and plums. Many of the trees were in blossom, and the scent was heavy in the morning air.

He could hear cockerels crowing, and dogs barking. Yelten was waking up, and everyone would try to do as much work as possible before the main heat of the day.

Aly touched heels to Okba's ribs, and the horse broke into a trot. It was impossible to ride in a straight line through the oasis, for the pathways followed the boundaries of the various gardens, and these were walled in. Aly's progress was a zig-zag affair, by a succession of right-angled turnings.

Here and there was an irrigation ditch which had to be jumped. It was Okba's habit to cat-jump such obstacles, and it was as he landed on the farther side of one of these channels that something whizzed over a nearby wall and caught Aly on the side of the head.

It was an unripe orange, and it knocked his turban askew, almost sending him from the saddle. Angrily, he pulled over to the wall, and shouted: "I see you!"

As a matter of truth, he saw nobody, for the culprit had immediately ducked under cover of some fruit bushes. All Aly had seen was the flicker of a brown arm as it showed above the wall. Unless he climbed over, he would never find out who was among those bushes, and he had no time for that. He guessed that his attacker was Musa, or Sami, the son of the Caid's cook. It was infuriating, and his head rang from the blow, but he dared not delay. What he had to report could not wait. It could be a matter of life or death for many in Yelten.

Muttering under his breath, he rode on, and around the next corner came upon Ibrahim, the blind man, having a waterskin filled from a well by his small daughter. Ibrahim sold water by the cup in the market place to those who were thirsty, charging them a small copper coin for the service. That was his way of making a living. He was desperately poor.

Before Aly could call a greeting, the blind man turned and exclaimed: "That is Aly ben Rabah! I know the step of Okba. You are early astir this morning, Aly."

"I have just ridden in from the desert with important news for the Caid. I cannot stay to talk, Ibrahim. I will see you later."

"Wait!" The blind man turned his pale, patient face. "Have you not heard? You will not find the Caid there."

"Why not?" demanded Aly. "I have been away two days, and have heard nothing. What has happened?"

"Yesterday the Caid was taken ill with severe pains, and the doctor could do nothing for him. They took him to Biskra in the motor machine that he so seldom uses. Hamed, his nephew, returned last night to say that he is in the French hospital to have an operation. We will pray that the foreign doctor knows what he is doing."

Aly was horrified. Such an eventuality had not occurred to him. He remembered that several times lately the Caid had complained of pains in his side.

"But I must see him!" he cried. "There is danger—much danger for Yelten. Who is taking his place?"

"Hamed is the only member of the family there, but he is not much good except for eating!" It was the truth. The nephew was a youth of nineteen, enormously fat, and given to gluttony. "But what is the danger you mention, Aly?"

"There are madmen at large with guns in their hands,

and murder in their hearts. They are from the legion of foreigners, but they are not French."

Rapidly, he told Ibrahim about the deserters and of how he had marooned them in Ain Zara. The blind man looked grave.

"You must go at once to the house and tell this to Hamed," he said. "He is the only one in Yelten who can drive the Caid's machine. He must go quickly to Biskra and get help."

Aly nodded, and again touched heels to Okba. It was more than forty miles to Biskra, the nearest town where there was a garrison. The Caid had only recently purchased an automobile and had brought his nephew from Algiers to drive it for him. It was true that there were no roads suitable for motor traffic around Yelten, but the track to Biskra was just possible, and beyond that town there were good roads to the coast. The Caid made use of his new purchase on his rare visits to Constantine or Algiers.

Aly clattered up to the gateway at such speed that the two guards ran out in alarm, reaching for their swords.

"Open the gate!" he cried. "I must see Hamed at once. There is grave news."

They thought he was referring to the Caid's illness and threw the gate wide. He was out of the saddle as soon as he was inside, leaving Okba standing in the shade as he ran across the terrace that led to the inner courtyard.

They did not rise early in the Caid's household. Few of the servants were astir. Someone was lighting the fire in the big kitchen. A manservant barred the way.

"I must speak with Hamed!" panted Aly.

"Hamed sleeps. He supped late last night after he returned from Biskra, and he is tired," grunted the other.

"Waken him!" exclaimed Aly. "I have bad news. Waken him!"

Impressed, the servant led him to the cool chamber

where Hamed snored noisily midst a pile of cushions on a divan. He had lost his desert simplicity since he had lived a soft life in Algiers and Paris. In his yellow silk underwear he was a monstrous sight as he stirred and groaned.

"What is it?" he asked, testily, without opening his eyes. "Is it news of my uncle?"

"No, Sidi!" said Aly, stepping forward. "It is news of evil men who will come here killing and looting. It would be well if you drove to Biskra and got help."

Hamed heaved his fat bulk to a sitting position.

"What are you saying?"

Aly related his encounter with the eight deserters from the Legion, and told how he had left them in Ain Zara. By the time he had finished Hamed had shrouded himself in a robe of the finest silk, and was pushing his feet into ornamental slippers.

"They may never come here!" he objected.

"They must come here to get water and supplies, Sidi," insisted Aly. "There is nowhere else for them to go. They dare not go to Biskra, and the mountains are too far for their tired camels. They will want your uncle's horses."

"But they will know you have warned us by now," protested Hamed, who did not want to believe that there was any real danger. "They will not dare come here!"

"These men would not care if we were ready for them. They know there are no soldiers in Yelten, and they know our guns are of no account. They have many guns of the latest type, and much ammunition. They could cut us down like reeds if we tried to fight them alone. They will not think we can get help from Biskra quickly, for they do not know about the Caid's motor machine."

Hamed screwed up his fat, white face as though he was about to cry.

"Why have I got to make that terrible journey to Biskra again? It bumped me to pieces last time. I am bruised from head to foot! Why am I the only one in Yelten who can drive? Besides, how can these men find their way here? You say you gave them a false trail."

"I did, Sidi, as far as I was able, but that sergeant is no fool. They will follow my tracks as far as the 'sea of stones', then they will know I must have turned north. They will find their way here. It may take them longer, Sidi, but they will surely come."

Hamed groaned afresh. He knew that Aly was right. He must drive to Biskra as quickly as possible, and summon assistance.

He called to a young manservant named Shulqani to accompany him, and went out to the empty stable where the vehicle was garaged. Shortly afterwards Aly saw it lurching and bumping along the track which led out of the oasis to the north.

Only then did he feel satisfied that he had done his duty. He was dizzy with fatigue and hunger but remembered that he must see to Okba before attending to his own wants. He led the stallion to the stable, rubbed it down, saw that it had water, and left it munching a big ration of oats.

By this time word had spread of the news which he had brought, and the entire staff of the Caid's household crowded around as he ate, to question him and to be given fuller details of the danger which threatened.

Some of them at once rushed off to hide their families and their valuables. Others prepared the big house against attack, closing heavy shutters over the windows, and barricading the lower doorways. The household guards, mostly elderly men, looked to their weapons, and wished there was someone to give them orders.

When he had eaten, Aly fell asleep in the kitchen, but he was roused by the arrival of his brother, Yusuf, who had guessed from the arrival of Fellah that he was there.

"We must send men to the south and east to keep watch

for these raiders," declared Yusuf. "If they come before the soldiers from Biskra arrive, we must meet them at the wadi and hold them back!"

They were brave words, but Aly wondered how long they could stand against trained men armed with modern weapons.

"Go home and rest," continued his brother. "Our mother and Mamouna are anxious about you. I will see that all is done that can be done, and we will send you word when the men are sighted."

Aly nodded sleepily. Now that his part was finished, reaction had set in, and he could hardly control his legs as he began to walk to his home. By this time the news had spread through the entire oasis, and on all sides he saw people either preparing to barricade themselves in their homes, or getting ready to flee northwards. At a time like this they needed the Caid to tell them what to do for the best. He could not have developed appendicitis at a worse time.

Aly avoided the market square because he did not want to be mobbed by questioners. He took a short cut through the palmery, and was halfway home when he met an old man named Fawzi, who was hurrying in the opposite direction. Fawzi was a date-grower who lived nearby. He clutched at Aly's shoulder, and demanded: "Is it true that those evil men are in Ain Zara?"

"It is true. I left them there last night, and escaped from them an hour before dawn."

The old man lifted his hands in horror.

"My son! Khami—my son—!"

Khami was about the same age as Aly.

"What about him?"

"He has gone to Ain Zara with Selim the donkey boy to fetch a load of wood. I have offered to buy it from Selim, and Khami has gone to help him," wailed Fawzi.

Aly stiffened, forgetting his weariness.

"When did they leave? How long have they been gone?"

"They left an hour before dawn, so that they could cover most of the journey before it became too hot. Do you think they will meet those men?"

Aly considered quickly. It was unlikely that the deserters would have set out on his trail before daylight. For one thing they would not be able to see his tracks until then, and for another both they and their camels had been exhausted when they had arrived at Ain Zara. Dawn was the earliest they would leave the dying oasis, and if Selim and Khami had travelled fast they would arrive there soon afterwards.

If anything had delayed the boys they might not yet have reached Ain Zara If they blundered unsuspectingly into the infuriated deserters they would be in grave danger, but first the sergeant would force them to tell him the shortest way to Yelten. He might even make one of them guide him to the oasis.

They could be already on the way! Everything depended on the speed at which Selim and his companion had travelled. Aly knew that he must find out for certain what was happening.

"I will try and stop Khami!" he told the agitated father, then turned and ran back to the Caid's house.

Miraculously, he no longer felt tired.

7 The Lookout Tower

He had put Okba at a gallop as soon as they crossed the wadi. Six miles of desert lay between them and Ain Zara, but Aly expected to know the worst when he had gone halfway, for there was a hillock with an old lookout tower, and from there he would be able to see the remainder of the track ahead. If Sergeant Hummel and his men were on their way, he should see them.

He had left the Caid's household in a state of panic. The news he had brought about Selim and Khami had thrown everyone into confusion.

By this time Fawzi would have told everyone in the market place, and there would be another stream of fugitives fleeing north, people who would not risk remaining to face the deserters.

Yusuf had sent out men on horseback to watch for them. Aly could see one of these scouts silhouetted on top of a dune to the west.

Despite the fact that it had rested little more than an hour, the stallion was as fresh as ever.

"We have no time to be tired," observed Aly, "but it is good to know that Hamed is on his way to Biskra. If he drives fast he will soon be there."

They slowed to cross a belt of pebbly shale, but galloped again as soon as conditions allowed. Ahead there was no sign of life. The old lookout stood against the brassy sky, for the sun had climbed high. It was already very hot.

They reached the foot of the hill. There was only one pathway to the top. Aly had always gone up there on foot, but now he set Okba at the steep climb. Slipping and floundering, dislodging loose stones and pieces of rock, the gallant horse went up in a series of short bounds. Aly pulled up behind the ruined tower; he did not want to show himself.

The tower had massive walls of great thickness, but the roof had long since fallen in. He climbed over the rubble inside, and peered from one of the narrow slit windows.

The glare from the desert was dazzling, but Ain Zara stood out clearly in the white light. He could see every yard of the faint track that led to the oasis. It wound between high, ridged dunes which ran like waves across the barren countryside. In places the dunes were a hundred feet high, but he could see over them. He could see three small figures about to descend into the old river bed.

They were two boys and a donkey. They had not yet entered Ain Zara. Something had delayed them.

He rushed back to Okba. There was still a chance of stopping Selim and his companion before they entered the ruined village. They were not moving fast.

He gained the saddle and sent Okba down the hillside. There was no time to follow the pathway. Snorting with indignation, the stallion commenced the dizzy descent, slithering and sliding, sometimes sitting down. Loose earth and sand formed a miniature land-slide before them. Aly kept his weight well back, and held his breath. He was putting his confidence in the exceptional sure-footedness of his mount.

They arrived at the bottom in a cloud of dust, and without being pressed the stallion set off at a gallop along the well-defined track.

The towering dunes now hid the oasis from their sight. Zig-zagging between these, skidding in the deep sand, they

kept up the mad speed until finally they shot onto the open approach to the dried-up river.

The boys and the donkey were toiling up the other side. The donkey had gone lame, which explained their slowness.

"Selim!" yelled Aly, but his voice was hoarse, cracked, and feeble. "Selim!"

The donkey boy heard him, and turned to see Aly waving wildly.

The river bed was a hundred yards across at that point. Aly cleared his throat, and yelled again: "Come back! There are men in the village who will kill you. Come back!"

"What do you say?" came the faint voice of Selim.

"Come back! Leave the donkey. Danger—!" bellowed Aly, pointing ahead.

Selim still hesitated, not yet understanding. It was Khami who first sensed the urgency in Aly's voice and started back down the slope so quickly that he lost his footing and rolled the rest of the way. Selim looked helplessly at his little donkey, which had begun to nibble at some thorn bushes, then he turned and followed Khami. It was a great wrench for him to leave the donkey, for he loved it dearly. It was his sole possession, his only "family".

Aly was watching the withered palms behind them, expecting the deserters to appear, but when at last he saw movement it was away to the east of the oasis, in the direction he had ridden out before dawn. A man on a camel had appeared on a ridge, and was looking in their direction. He raised a rifle and fired a shot into the air, doubtless as a signal to the rest of the party.

Selim and Khami heard the shot, and saw the man urging the camel towards them. They ran their hardest to Aly, who waited for them at the edge of the wadi.

Other camels now appeared over the distant ridge.

There were shouts. Aly and his horse had been recognized.

"Who are they?" panted Selim, as he reached his friend.

"Deserters from the Legion of foreigners. They are bad men, and they seek to go to Yelten to kill and steal. But help is coming from Biskra. We must get back."

Okba could not carry the three of them. Selim, who was thin and light, scrambled up behind Aly, while Khami ran alongside, hanging onto a stirrup.

Seeing that they were making off, the nearest pursuer beat his camel with his rifle butt, and the poor brute stumbled. Its long legs splayed in different directions, and it crashed head first, throwing its rider heavily.

Aly grunted with satisfaction. One of the other men stopped and opened fire with a rifle, but the range was extreme, and the bullets fell short.

Selim looked back sadly.

"My donkey—!"

"You can fetch it when all this is over," Aly told him. "It will find plenty to live on in Ain Zara. It could not have kept up with us."

He went on to explain fully about the men who were trying to overtake them, and he made his companions understand that they could expect no mercy if they were captured.

There was little fear of the camels catching up with them, but their riders only had to follow the boys and they would be led to Yelten. There was no way of avoiding this. The only consolation was that help should be arriving soon from Biskra.

Khami was getting out of breath, and they had to slow down. Selim offered to change places with him. The other boy was stubborn and said that he could carry on, but it was soon evident that he could not do this. He had a weak chest, and began to cough.

They were almost level with the watch-tower. The camels were about a mile behind, hidden by a dip in the ground. Aly rode in among the boulders at the foot of the hill and dropped from the saddle, exclaiming: "Take the reins, Selim! Get up behind him, Khami."

"But you—?" began the date-grower's son.

"I will hide until they are past, then follow on foot. Ride hard, Selim, and keep well ahead, then these men will not notice that there are only two of you. Tell them in Yelten that the deserters are on their way. Perhaps you will find the soldiers from Biskra already there."

Okba looked bewildered when he saw his master was being left behind. Aly patted him, and gave him a push.

"Go, Okba! Go, and I will follow!"

Tossing its head doubtfully, the stallion broke into a gallop, and Aly watched from behind a boulder. He believed he had done the right thing. He was tougher and stronger than the others, and better fitted to travel on foot.

The camels were now drawing nearer. There were only six between the eight men. The others had been lost or had collapsed.

Sergeant Hummel led the way on a big, beige camel which looked as angry as its rider. None of the party knew how to handle camels correctly, and they were all having trouble. These were not riding camels, but draught beasts accustomed to carrying heavy loads at no more than three miles an hour. The Germans were vainly trying to hurry them.

The men were in savage mood. They had found no water in Ain Zara, and they were very thirsty. They could see the cloud of dust which marked the rapid progress of Okba, and they now knew the direction in which Yelten lay.

Someone suggested that there might be water under the old watch-tower. Some of these ancient strongholds had cisterns cut in the rock below them. Aly was startled to see the party suddenly turn in his direction. He hurriedly got under cover, and watched warily.

Sergeant Hummel was trying to persuade his comrades not to waste time. He said that even if there were cisterns, they would almost certainly be dry, but the thirst-crazed men refused to listen to him. They slid from their camels and started to climb the hill.

The sergeant refused to accompany them, and sat his loudly complaining camel no more than a dozen yards from where Aly was hidden. He was looking worried. He had several days' growth of beard, and as it was light gold, it framed his gaunt face in fantastic fashion. His eyes were bloodshot, and he was in a foul temper. When his camel tried to move towards a thorn bush, he beat it on the head with the butt of his revolver.

"Hurry!" he bellowed to those on the hill. "Why waste time? You'll find no water."

Excited shouts came from those at the top. Some of them were pointing to the west. Aly could not understand what they were saying, but Hummel urged his camel round to the other side of the hill, and the others raced down the pathway from above at breakneck speed. They had seen something in the distance.

Aly crawled from rock to rock until he could also see what was happening. A string of laden camels was approaching along a track which passed close to the watch-tower. They were about a mile distant, with a number of Arabs trudging beside them. It was a caravan from one of the southern oases, on its way to Yelten market with produce. Aly recognized it as belonging to an elderly merchant named Athras, who had a young son, Zeheli.

The deserters had stopped shouting. They were getting under cover, and had unslung their rifles. Hummel had dismounted, and was giving orders in a low voice.

The camel caravan would have food and water. The deserters were going to attack it and take what they wanted.

Aly realized this with horror. The unsuspecting Arabs were getting nearer every moment. They wanted to reach Yelten before the mid-morning heat, little knowing what danger awaited them in the shadow of the watch-tower.

"I must do something to stop this!" decided Aly.

He looked about him desperately. The sergeant and the others were out of sight. The only one who had not hidden himself was the burly Pole, who had been left with the camels on the eastern side of the hill.

Aly looked at Polskie and the camels. They were standing in a group in a patch of desert scrub. They were nibbling at this contentedly, grateful for the brief rest. The Pole had seated himself on a boulder, where he could keep an eye on them. He had taken off one of his boots and was attending to a blister on his foot.

Aly crawled past him, and reached the windward side of the grazing camels. There was only a light breeze, hot and dust-laden, but it was enough for his purpose. In his pocket he had a box of matches. These had not often come his way for they cost money, and poor desert dwellers employed other means to light their fires. But since he had become a part of the Caid's household he had been able to supply his family with matches. These were intended for his mother.

He wriggled behind a clump of the spiky, grey-green bushes, and struck two of the matches. The shrubs caught at once, for they were tinder-dry. The flames rose high, were fanned by the wind, and leapt to the next bush.

Aly rolled back into a shallow gully, and lay still.

There was a sudden grunt from the Pole. The smell of smoke had caused him to turn, and by that time several of the bushes were blazing. The fire was spreading rapidly. Shouting in alarm, Polskie ran forward with the idea of beating out the flames.

By then the smoke had enveloped the camels. They raised their heads and saw the flames devouring the scrub

CP

faster than even they could have done. Bellowing in panic, they turned and stampeded.

Polskie made a dash for the leading beast, and grabbed its dangling head rope. Such was his strength that he hauled it to a standstill, but a fresh cloud of smoke caused the terrified camel to snap at his hand. He let go, roaring with pain.

The noise was heard by the others. One of them came running to see what was happening. He found Polskie sucking his bleeding hand, while the camels scattered towards the horizon.

His cries brought the rest of the party. Some raced after the camels, whilst the others tried to throw sand on the spreading flames.

Under cover of the smoke, Aly slipped round to the other side of the hill and ran towards the camel-train. The Arabs had seen the smoke, and heard the uproar. They had halted.

Aly raced towards them, every moment expecting to hear the crack of a rifle, and to feel the impact of a bullet.

8 Terror Comes to Yelten

Okba gave no trouble. Selim hung onto the reins grimly when the stallion got into its stride, and Khami clung on behind, pale, for he was not accustomed to such riding.

"Truly he seems to have wings!" muttered the donkey boy. "No wonder Aly is proud of him. Can you see him yet?"

Several times Khami looked back, but reported that he could see no one following. When he glanced back for the last time before they descended into the wadi outside Yelten, he exclaimed: "I see smoke! There is a fire."

Selim pulled up, and they watched the dark column of smoke that rose near the watch-tower. They knew that the scrub must be burning.

"I do not understand what it means, but be sure Aly had a hand in it!" said Selim. "Come, we must warn everyone that these men are on their way."

They hurried across the wadi. Usually there was a noisy crowd of boys and girls at the waterhole, but now it was deserted. Life was not normal in Yelten that morning.

As they climbed the steep track on the other side they were hailed by two men who were watching from beneath the palms.

"Ho, there, Selim! Where is Aly ben Rabah, and why are you riding his horse?"

They were members of the Caid's household, and both had ancient rifles. They were part of Yelten's pitiful defence force.

"He follows on foot. He sent us ahead to warn that the foreign deserters are on their way. They cannot be far behind us," Selim told them. "Where are the soldiers from Biskra?"

"They will not be coming," growled one of the men. "Shulqani, who went with Hamed, returned an hour ago to say that they ran into a ditch not many miles away, and Hamed is injured."

Selim stared blankly. This was the worst possible news. Aly had expected help from Biskra by this time, but because of this accident news of the deserters would not have got through. Some of the fugitives from Yelten would reach Biskra eventually, but not for many hours. Help could not come until the following day. Meantime Yelten was open to any attack.

Khami gave a yelp of dismay, dropped from the horse, and fled through the palms to find his father.

"We are to guard the path," said the elder man. "Go, Selim, to the Caid's house. Some of the elders are gathered there. Tell them what you have told us."

Selim wasted no time. The gardens were deserted. No one was at work that morning. Those who had not fled were either in hiding or had gone to the Caid's house.

He found the courtyard crowded. The priest was there, the schoolmaster, and the doctor, but it was Ibrahim, the blind water seller, who was the most prominent. He broke off an impassioned speech as Selim came clattering through the gate.

"It is Okba!" he cried, recognizing the hoof beats. "What news, Aly?"

"It is Selim who rides Okba," someone told him, and the donkey boy shouted the news as he slid from the saddle.

Immediately there was uproar.

"We are lost! We must flee!" cried the doctor. "We shall all be murdered!"

"Wait!" implored the blind man, clutching his sleeve. "Where shall we flee? It is forty miles to Biskra, and there is no water on the way. Those who have gone ahead did not take much with them. They will be suffering from heat and thirst. We would be mad to do likewise."

"But these foreigners are dangerous animals!" protested another. "They will shoot on sight. What can we do against them? How can we protect our women and children?"

"Listen!" urged Ibrahim. "We cannot fight them. We will hide the women and children in the water cisterns under the old fort. We will hide our weapons so that these men will not be made angry by seeing them. When they come I will go out to meet them alone, and will tell them that they can have what they want in the way of food and horses if they do us no harm. I shall tell them we are men of peace."

"They will shoot you, Ibrahim!" asserted the teacher.

The blind man shrugged.

"If it is Allah's will, I shall be shot, but I think that when they see I am blind and helpless they will listen to me. I am willing to do this thing."

The argument continued. Selim left them and led Okba to the stables, where he unsaddled him and rubbed him down. Then he supplied the horse with fresh water and oats.

When he turned from doing this, Sami was beside him.

"Why is Aly not with his horse?" asked the cook's son.

Selim told him, and added that Aly would be back before long. Sami nodded.

"Then I will look after Okba until he comes. You must be hungry, Selim. The kitchen is empty. Go and help yourself."

Selim was ravenous. It was an invitation that he could

not resist. He knew nothing of Sami's feelings for Aly.

The stable boy waited until he was out of sight, then untied Okba and led him quietly out by the other door, through the deserted courtyard at the back, and so into the palm groves.

There was a great deal of noise in the front courtyard. A decision was being made about Ibrahim's plan.

Sami led the stallion across the oasis, keeping out of sight of everyone. In any case, they were much too concerned with their own troubles to notice what he was doing. Okba twice tried to turn back. He did not trust this boy who spoke to him softly and offered him dates.

Finally Sami brought him to the eastern edge of the oasis, and there turned him loose.

"Go!" he cried, and lashed the horse across the quarters with a long, whippy palm-frond.

Okba kicked up his heels and galloped away, tossing his head and snorting. It was a long time since he had been free, and the experience was not unpleasant.

Sami stood in the shade of the palms and watched the white stallion disappear over a ridge. He grinned as he turned.

"That's the last Aly will see of his wonderful Okba! He will soon find he is no one of importance. He cannot run to the Caid for help, and the Caid may die in hospital, then Aly will be nobody again!"

Very pleased with himself, he went to the market place to hear the latest news. He did not fear the coming of the deserters, for he knew of a safe hiding place.

Meantime the elders had agreed to adopt Ibrahim's plan. While watch was kept to the south, the women and small children were collected and hurried to the old fort. For many years this had been in ruins, but there had been a time when it had withstood long sieges by the enemies of Yelten before the French had brought peace to the land.

These days the children played among the ruins, and

the great cisterns cut out of the rock below were dark, empty caverns, frequented only by scorpions, beetles, and bats.

The entrance was well hidden, and through this now passed more than a hundred women and children and a few aged men. They had some food, waterskins, and such possessions as they had been able to carry with them. They would not be comfortable, but they would be out of the way of the wild foreigners who would soon be rampaging through the oasis.

They were scarcely under cover when word came that the raiders were approaching. As they came nearer it was seen that there were eight men and three camels. The other camels had eluded capture after the stampede.

The Yelten men watched from well back among the palms as the group reached the other side of the wadi. The camels smelled water and would have rushed down to the pool, but the men held them back while they scanned the edge of the oasis for signs of danger. At an order from Hummel someone sprayed the palms with bullets. An elderly Arab was wounded. The rest fled to the mosque, and crowded inside.

Sergeant Hummel decided that it was safe to descend to the pool. There his men beat back the camels until they had slaked their own thirst, but the sergeant stopped them from drinking too much.

"We'll find something better than water in the village," he told them. "Wait, who is this coming?"

A solitary figure was descending the pathway towards them, tapping the ground with his stick. It was Ibrahim, and in his other hand he carried a white cloth which he waved as token of his peaceful intentions.

Someone raised a rifle, but Hummel knocked it aside.

"Let us hear what the old man has to say," he grunted.

Ibrahim knew the risk he was taking, but came on

boldly, calling out: "Welcome! I would speak with the Sidi in charge."

"Speak up, and make it short!" barked Hummel.

"Sidi, we of Yelten are men of peace, and we make you welcome," said Ibrahim. "You have come far, and you must be tired and hungry. We have food, mint tea, and coffee. All is at your disposal. No one will stand in your way."

"They had better not try!" growled the sergeant. "We are men without patience, and we will water your palms with your own blood if you give us trouble. How many men are here?"

"Less than a hundred, Sidi. The others have fled with the women and children. We who remain have no guns. Our hands are empty."

"And how long is it since you sent word to Biskra that we were coming?" demanded the sergeant.

"It will be many hours before the news reaches Biskra," Ibrahim assured him. "All that we ask is that you take what you want and go in peace. We are poor men, but we offer all we have, and—"

Hummel stepped forward and swung his fist. The speaker dropped to the ground like a half-filled sack.

"You are giving us nothing, old fool, for we take what we want!" snarled Hummel. He added to his companions, "Come on, but keep your fingers on the triggers. At the first sign of trouble, open fire!"

They hurried up the pathway, leaving Ibrahim unconscious, for he had struck his head on a stone.

At the top they fanned out and advanced through the gardens with their guns at hip-level, eight grim, dusty figures with murder in their eyes. They were no longer soldiers, but human wolves, ready to do anything to retain their misbegotten liberty. Several of them had been criminals before they had joined the Legion. Now they were all outside the law.

Something moved under the palms, and there was a burst of gunfire. A lone donkey squealed in its death agony, and fell at the end of the rope which tethered it.

"Steady!" warned Hummel. "Don't waste shots!"

They advanced up the Street of the Olive Trees, noting that the doors of the humble homes were open, and that they were all empty. They came to the market place, and men ran to each side-passage with rifle at the ready.

There was still no sign of life. There were food shops, but they were shuttered. Someone suggested breaking them open, but the sergeant had noticed a movement in the doorway of the mosque, and he strode towards it with a revolver in his fist.

"Come out, or I open fire!" he commanded.

The tall, pale-faced teacher came forward and protested in voluble French that they wished only to be friends.

"Then tell the others to show themselves," ordered Hummel.

The teacher spoke, and everyone filed from the building, young men and old, youths, and a few small boys. They were scared of these gaunt scarecrows in tattered uniforms, but they tried not to show it. Some of them would have preferred to fight.

"Where is your Caid?" thundered Hummel.

"He was taken ill, Sidi, and is in Biskra hospital," the teacher told him.

"So that is why you act like mice instead of men!" jeered Hummel. "Well, perhaps you are wise! Open up these shops, and bring food to the Caid's house, for we shall be staying there. Hurry!"

He fired a shot over their heads, and they scattered to do his bidding, opening doors and shutters, and bringing out the choicest things in the shops.

"Lead the way to the Caid's house," ordered the sergeant, when he was satisfied that they had enough food to supply an army. "While you cook for us we will see what horses the Caid has in his stables."

His orders were obeyed. Everything was carried to the Caid's house, and Sami's father was given the task of preparing a gigantic meal for the hungry visitors.

Some of the deserters were so tired that they would have dropped down to sleep on the cushioned divans in the outer hall, but Hummel would not allow that. He made the giant Pole responsible for keeping them awake, and forced a member of the staff to accompany him as he toured the building.

He saw many things of value, but he knew they could not be burdened with heavy loot. He realized that news of their presence in Yelten would soon reach Biskra. He intended to be gone before troops could be rushed to round them up.

With good horses and supplies they stood a fair chance of reaching the Tunisian border. If they could cross that they would be safe, for the Tunisians were at loggerheads with the French Government, and had undertaken to repatriate to their own countries any deserters from the Legion who sought asylum in Tunisia.

However, Franz Hummel did not intend to leave empty handed. In the Caid's bed-chamber he turned and thrust the muzzle of his gun into the stomach of the elderly manservant.

"Where does the Caid keep his jewels and money?" he demanded.

The Arab turned grey.

"I know not, Sidi!" he gasped. "He tells no one."

"So, he tells no one!" snarled the sergeant, prodding harder. "I guarantee there is not one of you who does not know. Speak, you misshapen ape, or I'll blow a hole in your stomach!"

The man looked into the German's cruel eyes, and faltered:

"There is a chest—"

"Show me!"

He was led to a small ante-chamber where stood a huge, iron-studded chest with a massive lock of ancient pattern. Such treasure chests were found in the homes of most wealthy Arabs.

There was no key, but Hummel did not require one. He suddenly raised his revolver and clubbed the old Arab, dropping him unconscious and bleeding to the floor. Then he fired two shots into the lock, shattering it. The heavy lid lifted readily.

When he left the room his pockets bulged with several hundred thousand francs in notes, and with jewels in old-fashioned settings. He knew that without the settings the diamonds and rubies would be worth a fortune. This was the nest egg that he intended taking with him into Tunisia.

The shots brought one of the other men running to see what was happening. Hummel met him outside the door.

"It's all right, Kurt," he said, calmly. "That fool of a guide tried to lock me in a cupboard, so I rubbed him out. Come with me and look at the stables. There ought to be some good horse-flesh in a place like this."

They went down a back staircase and across the courtyard to the stables. There they found more than a score of fine horses. Their transport problem was solved, but Hummel went up and down the line of stalls, peering at each animal, and finally grunting: "The white stallion—the one ridden by the boy who fooled us—it's not here. I fancied it for myself."

"It would have been a tired horse, and these others are fresh," pointed out Kurt.

The sergeant nodded agreement, and they hastened back to find that the meal was ready to be served.

"Eat your fill," Hummel told the others, "for we won't have much time for eating on the journey."

"We're not leaving yet!" protested someone. "Surely we can stay till nightfall?"

"No! Every hour we stay here increases our chances of being caught. There are fine horses in the stable, more than enough for our needs. We'll be able to carry some hostages along with us."

"Hostages!" exclaimed his listeners, for it was the first they had heard of this idea.

"Yes, we need hostages. The authorities may send out planes or helicopters to hunt us when they hear we're making for the border. Ever heard of machine guns? Do you want to be shot up from the air? No! So we'll take along a dozen or so hostages. It would have been better if we'd had women and children, but as they've sent those away we'll have to make do with some of the men. Airmen will think twice about firing on us if they see us mixed up with a bunch of civilians. Get the idea?"

They agreed that it was a splendid plan.

9 Treachery!

Aly motioned to his companion to be cautious as they neared the edge of the wadi. They lay behind a boulder and studied the oasis on the other side.

The boy with him was Zeheli, the son of Ahras, the merchant whose camels he had seen from the watch-tower. He had succeeded in reaching them and warning Ahras of what awaited them.

Ahras had at once suggested turning due north, and proceeding directly to Biskra, by-passing Yelten, but Aly had persuaded him to remain halted while Zeheli and he made their way to the oasis to see what had happened there. Zeheli was to take the news back to his father. He was about Aly's age, but shorter, more powerfully built, with the thick calves of one who had tramped beside camels since an early age. He wore a cotton robe, a pair of heavy sandals, and nothing else. His heavier garments were on one of the camels, and were donned only when it turned colder at night.

They were tired, hot, and dusty. They could see the pool glimmering below them, but Aly hesitated to go down.

"I cannot understand why everything is so quiet," he muttered. "I thought we should have seen the soldiers from Biskra, or their patrol cars."

"Perhaps they have come and gone. Perhaps they have

taken the deserters away with them," suggested Zeheli.

"Then why are none of my people at the pool? Why is nobody working in the gardens? I do not like it. We will go down and drink, but be careful."

They made their way to the waterhole and slaked their thirst. There was still no sound from the palm groves. Aly felt uneasy. It was not what he had expected.

As they moved away towards the pathway to the top, they heard low groans. Aly saw something stirring beside one of the boulders. A man was trying to sit up, holding his head.

"Ibrahim!" gasped the boy. "What has happened?"

The blind man turned and grabbed his arm, while Zeheli looked on open-mouthed.

"Do not show yourself!" warned Ibrahim. "The deserters are here, and I do not know what has been happening since I was knocked unconscious. I do not know how long I have lain here."

"You mean the soldiers from Biskra did not get here in time?"

"No, the message never reached them. Hamed had an accident," groaned Ibrahim.

Aly was staggered. Things could not have been worse. Between them they got the old man to the pool, where he bathed his head and drank deeply. Then he told them all that had happened, how the women and children were hidden in the ancient cisterns, and how he had persuaded the men not to fight.

"We would have stood no chance," he insisted. "I thought only of preventing bloodshed, and there was no one to lead us."

Aly agreed that this was so, although his instincts rebelled against giving in tamely to the raiders.

"Mamounah—and my mother?" he asked.

"They will have gone with the others to the old fort, and there they must stay until these evil men have gone away, which will be soon. They will take the Caid's horses and go."

"They will take the Caid's horses—" repeated Aly, and then remembered Okba. "My horse—what did Selim do with it?"

"I do not know. He was riding it when he arrived, but after we heard his news there was much argument and I do not know where he went. No doubt he took Okba to the stables."

Aly groaned.

"Then that sergeant will take him!"

He felt that all was lost. Nothing worse could happen to him. It was Zeheli who reminded him of other things.

"I must go back to my father and tell him not to come here," he said.

"But he is short of water, and the camels will never reach Biskra without a drink," pointed out Aly. "Here is the only water. Ibrahim is right. These men cannot afford to stay here long. Before morning they will have gone, and it will be safe for your father to bring the caravan here. Go and tell him this."

Zeheli turned away; Aly took the blind man's arm.

"I will help you to the top of the pathway, then I must go and see what is happening at the Caid's house," he said.

They toiled slowly up the steep slope, for Ibrahim's legs were very feeble, but once he was among the palms he bade Aly be gone, saying that he could fend for himself. Despite his blindness, he knew every inch of the oasis.

Aly raced through the gardens, all fatigue forgotten in his eagerness to know what had happened to his horse. He took short cuts, climbed over boundary walls, and trampled through growing crops, but he met no one. He passed within fifty yards of his home, but did not go there because he knew that his mother and sister were with the other women folk. He wondered what had happened to Fellah.

As he approached the Caid's house he saw that all the remaining men were squatting in the outer courtyard under the watchful eye of the big Pole, whose gun rested across the crook of a massive arm. Within the main hall a voice was raised in anger. It was the voice of Sergeant Hummel.

Aly did not enter the courtyard, but crept along the outside of the wall until he was opposite the stables. There he clambered over, and dropped among some bushes. There was no one in sight.

He ran to the stable door, and then straight to the stall where he kept Okba.

It was empty; there was some oats in the trough. Thinking that Selim may have put the stallion in another stall, he ran the length of the stables, looking everywhere. There were nearly twenty horses, but Okba was not one of them.

He pulled up at the other entrance, uncertain whether to be pleased or distressed. Selim had ridden Okba up to the house. He must have stabled Okba somewhere, but where? Had he hidden the stallion? The only way to settle that was to find Selim.

He went back to a spot where he could look down into the courtyard. He scanned the group of huddled figures, most of them squatting silently. He saw his brother, and others of his friends, but at first he did not see Selim. Finally he spied him in a far corner, sitting alone, looking miserable. Aly guessed he was thinking of the donkey which he had been obliged to leave in Ain Zara.

He circled the building outside the wall, and came up behind the corner where his friend sat. A fig tree gave cover, and he climbed up and looked over the wall.

"Selim!" he whispered. "Do not turn round! It is Aly. Can you hear me?"

Selim stiffened, but did not turn his head.

"I hear you, Aly. These men are getting ready to leave. They have looted the Caid's house."

"Where is Okba? What did you do with him after you arrived here?"

"I put him where he always stands in the stable, and saw that he had oats and water. Then I went to eat in the kitchen. These men came soon afterwards."

"Okba is not in the stables!" hissed Aly. "Did you tether him?"

Selim found it hard not to turn.

"I tied him with a long rope, as you do. He cannot have gone. Nobody has ridden him away from here, but these men are going to take the Caid's horses, and—"

There was an interruption. Hummel had appeared at the top of the steps leading down to the courtyard, with his men about him. They had draped Arab robes over their ragged uniforms. Most of them were laden with loot, and they were flushed with heavy eating. The sergeant scowled at the squatting crowd.

"On your feet!" he bellowed. "You'll be glad to know that we are leaving—but some of you are coming with us."

Impassive faces were turned to him. Aly peered over the wall in the shadow of the fig tree, and noted how the sergeant's pockets bulged, but he did not then know that Hummel carried with him a fortune in money and jewels.

At a nod from the sergeant his men began to herd the Arabs together. Selim was obliged to go with the rest. Aly lay flat on the top of the wall. He wondered what was going to happen.

Hummel walked up to the teacher, to the imam of the mosque, and to several other leading citizens.

"You are coming with us—and you—and you—!" he growled, pushing them to one side. "I want a dozen of you. If we die on the way to the border, so do you!"

Some of those in the background started to edge away. Aly noticed that one of these was Musa, the bully. Musa dodged out through the gateway.

One of the Germans saw him go, and shouted. Musa ran, the man after him.

"Stop, or I shoot!" The German raised his rifle as Musa fled beneath the wall on which Aly was hidden. "Stop!"

The threat terrified Musa. He fell to his knees just below Aly.

"Do not shoot, Sidi!" he pleaded.

"For this you are going with us, and you'll walk all the way!" raged the deserter, and he grabbed Musa by the nape of the neck and shook him violently.

"Mercy!" sobbed the youth. "Do not hurt me, and I will tell you something. All the women and children have not been sent away."

"What is that?" demanded his captor, changing his grip to Musa's throat. "What did you say?"

"The women and children—they are in the oasis—hidden!" panted Musa. "Let me go, and I will show you where they are. They are hidden under the old fort. I swear it!"

"Come with me!" growled the man, dragging him by the arm. "Hi, Sergeant!"

Sick with disgust, Aly saw the treacherous Musa dragged up to Sergeant Hummel, and heard him repeat what he had already said. An evil grin spread over Hummel's face.

"If this is true, it couldn't be better!" he chuckled. "Women and children make much better hostages than men. Nobody would dare fire on us if we had women and children with us. Two of you go with the boy and see if he tells the truth. If he has lied, shoot him!"

There was no time for Aly to run to the old fort with warning. He was compelled to remain where he was as Musa was taken away. Musa had betrayed the women and children to save his own skin. A red mist of rage dimmed Aly's eyes.

Inside the courtyard there was confusion. Some of the

men understood what was happening, and pleaded with the sergeant to take them instead of their families. He yelled for them to be silent, and when they persisted he fired shots over their heads, sending them cowering to the ground.

"Take some of them and make them saddle up the horses," he ordered. "Load four of the horses with water-skins. Any spare horses will be for the hostages."

Five minutes later one of the deserters came running back to report that the cisterns had been found to be crowded with women and children. Hummel showed his satisfaction by slapping the teacher on the back.

"Do you hear that? Now you won't have to make the journey. We'll collect the women as we pass the fort."

A long line of saddled horses was led from the stables. Some of them were laden with filled waterskins. The Germans were in high spirits as they mounted. Some of them led spare horses. When the sergeant was astride the Caid's own black charger, he turned to threaten the glowering Arabs.

"If you try to follow us we will kill your wives and daughters!" he promised.

No one saw Aly drop from the wall and make for the ruined fort. It was too late for him to do anything, but he wanted to see what happened there.

He arrived a little before the mounted men, and hid in some bushes to watch. One of the deserters was on guard at the entrance to the cisterns. Musa sprawled on the ground beside him, looking very frightened, and still babbling for mercy. His voice was almost drowned by the wailing of those inside. They knew they had been discovered, and expected to be massacred.

When Hummel arrived he told his men to dismount and line up on either side of the entrance. He then shouted for the women and children to come out.

Instead, they pressed back as far as they could into the

darkness. He had to send men inside to haul them out. Kicking and struggling, a score of them were dragged forth and made to mount the spare horses.

There were two or three to a horse, about equal numbers of women and girls. No care was taken that children were with their own mothers. They were tossed onto the horses, and were threatened with death if they dismounted.

The noise was ear-splitting. Not only did those scream who were being taken, but those left behind added to the pandemonium.

Aly almost left his hiding place when he saw that one of the last dragged through the doorway was his sister, Mamounah. A burly, bearded German had her by the arm, while her mother clung desperately to the other, begging him to let her daughter go. He pushed her in the face with his open hand to make her release her hold, then carried the kicking, struggling girl to a horse which already carried a woman and a child.

"Get up there, and stay there!" he ordered. "If you fall off I'll put a bullet in you."

It was hard for Aly to remain still while this was happening. Harder still was it to see the mounted foreigners lead their captives out of the oasis into the open desert. Everyone was crying. Those left in the cisterns came rushing out to see their friends and relatives carried away they knew not where. Their screams filled the air.

Musa had been left behind. He crawled out of the corner where he had been huddled, with the intention of running away, but Aly was waiting for him. He rushed at the bigger boy with whirling fists.

"Traitor! Betrayer of women and children!" he cried.

His blows rocked Musa back on his heels. Although much taller and heavier than Aly, he had no chance against the fury of the younger boy. Aly's hard head took him in the stomach, and down he went, with Aly on top of him, pummelling him with both fists.

He bellowed and roared for mercy, but Aly could only remember that his sister was being carried away into the desert, and he paid no heed to the other's cries. Musa's nose was flattened, and his lips were cut and bleeding, when strong hands gripped Aly and lifted him to his feet.

"Leave him, Aly," came his brother's voice. "We will deal with Musa."

There were other men with him, and they dragged the screaming youth away.

10 Aly Takes the Trail

Aly walked slowly away from his home. He had left his mother, overwrought at the loss of Mamounah, in the care of a friend. There was nothing more that he could do to comfort her.

Fellah had vanished during the confusion, and nobody knew where he had gone. Yusuf had ridden out with some of the men on a varied collection of camels and horses. Some of the latter had spent their entire lives drawing water from the wells, and could hardly raise a trot, but they were the only horses left in Yelten.

About thirty men were in this party following the raiders. They could not hope to overtake them, nor would they have dared to do so, lest the hostages should be killed, but they wanted to be close behind in case the women and children were abandoned.

To his great disgust Aly was not allowed to go with his brother. Only grown men with weapons made up the group.

He looked vainly for Selim. He guessed that Selim was mourning the loss of his donkey, just as he was mourning the disappearance of Okba. There was still no news of the stallion.

He walked to the edge of the wadi, and looked across the desert to the east. Far away in the distance he could see a cloud of dust, and knew that would be the deserters and their hostages. The pace they were maintaining would be a cruel ordeal for the women and children.

The fugitives were now disguised in Arab clothing. If they were seen from the air they would be taken for a party of Arabs travelling with their families. If, on the other hand, they were recognized, no airman would machine gun them when he saw who was with them.

Aly could see his brother's contingent several miles to the rear of the others. They were moving much more slowly.

Then, as he gloomily surveyed the scene before him, he saw something moving far down the wadi, half a mile beyond the pool. Some animal was coming in to drink.

"Selim's donkey!" was the thought that entered his head. "It has found its way back from Ain Zara."

But a few moments later he saw that it was too big for a donkey. It was a horse, light in colour. His heart bumped painfully as he leaned forward and strained his eyes.

"It can't be—I must be imagining things!" he gasped. "It—it is Okba!"

The stallion must have entered the wadi several miles to the east, and was now making for the waterhole.

Aly checked himself from jumping down the sheer face of the cliff. He ran to the top of the pathway, and went down this with the speed of a goat. It was a miracle that he did not fall, but he reached the bottom without mishap, and ran his hardest for the pool.

The stallion was already knee-deep in the water. It raised its head when he called its name, then went on drinking.

He waded out and threw his arms around its neck.

"Okba, you've come back! Okba—!" he repeated over and over again. "What happened to you? Where have you been?"

Okba blew noisily, then backed onto the coarse grass that grew around the pool, and submitted to a thorough examination. Now and then he thrust his wet nose at Aly as though to assure him that he was glad to be back.

Aly could find nothing wrong, except that he was streaked with dust and sweat. It was obvious that he had been galloping in the desert, but how had he got loose in the first place? The headstall was gone, and it was improbable that Okba had got rid of that himself. Someone had removed it and turned him loose! Someone had gone to the stable after Selim left.

"Sami!" decided Aly, remembering how the cook's son had introduced a snake into Okba's trough. "It must have been Sami. He was madly jealous of Okba. He thought he was spiting me by turning him loose, and all the time he was doing me a good turn!"

He laughed aloud, and Okba looked at him in astonishment. Aly was almost hysterical with relief. Sami had done him a great service by saving Okba from the German sergeant. But for Sami, the stallion would have been far away in the desert with the fugitives.

He led Okba back into the water and scrubbed him down with handfuls of grass. With more grass he dried him.

By that time the sun was setting. For most people the day was ending, but for Aly it was only just beginning. He had recovered Okba, and his confidence. Now he felt capable of facing anything. Already a plan was forming in his head. The deserters had several hours' start, but on Okba he could easily overtake them.

He took the stallion by the mane and led it to the top of the cliff, where he mounted and headed for the Caid's stables. Although he had neither saddle nor bridle, a touch of his heel or a tap from his hand was sufficient guidance.

The short twilight was ending as he rode through the oasis. He met nobody, but he heard loud wailing. The women folk were still mourning the loss of relatives and friends who had been taken away. They believed them gone forever.

There were no guards on the gateway to the Caid's residence, but a slim figure emerged from the kitchen and ran towards him. It was Selim, who had been enjoying another free meal.

"Aly—Okba—Where did you find him?"

"He came in from the desert to drink at the pool," explained Aly, as he slid to the ground. "When you took him to the stable was Sami about?"

"Yes. He said he would look after Okba."

"Ah-h!" His suspicions were confirmed. "It was he who turned Okba loose, but I cannot be angry with him. But for him Okba would be on his way to Tunisia!"

His face shone with happiness.

"What are you going to do?" asked the donkey boy, as they led the horse to the empty stables.

"I'm going to give him another feed, and let him rest until the moon comes up. Then I am going after Mamounah."

"But—" began Selim.

"I am going to rescue her, and the others too," went on Aly. "Then I shall try to stop them taking the Caid's horses into Tunisia."

His friend looked at him with awe.

"You will be too late," he faltered.

"No, it is seventy miles to the border, and even if they travel all night they will be only halfway by daylight. I shall take a gun. I know where the Caid keeps some very special guns which he bought in Algiers last month."

As he spoke he was attending to Okba, who did not appear to be unduly fatigued by his adventure.

"Let us get those guns, then I must sleep a little," continued Aly. "Waken me when the moon rises, Selim."

"Yes, but—but wouldn't it be wiser to ride to Biskra for help?"

"No! Word of these happenings will reach there before long, and the soldiers will come. But what can they do? By then those men will be halfway to the border, and even if airplanes are sent after them, they will not be able to stop them hiding behind the women and children. There must not be a fight while Mamounah and the others are in their hands. Once I have rescued them it will not matter if the airplanes swoop."

Selim nodded wonderingly, overawed by Aly's confidence. They were entering the house, which was almost in darkness.

"It is said that these men took away the Caid's treasure," murmured Selim. "Old Abdel was found dead beside the chest."

"That will have been the sergeant!" exclaimed Aly angrily, as he led the way to a hidden cabinet in a recess behind the divan where the Caid usually reclined.

The guns he had mentioned, with a supply of cartridges, were still there. When he had first bought them the Caid had treated them as new toys, and often Aly had watched him load them. Now he loaded both, and gave one to Selim.

"Watch over my mother while I am away," he said, "and if Fellah returns tie him up."

Selim nodded. He had never before handled a revolver, but he tucked it in his belt and paraded up and down while Aly slept on one of the divans.

In the village the remaining men had gathered in the mosque to discuss the situation. Darkness had closed down, and a faint breeze came from the north. The stars grew brighter, but later they would be out-shone by the rising moon.

In the stable Okba finished the oats. He was quite alone, for all his usual companions were on their way to Tunisia.

Selim was very tired. He found a pile of cushions, comfortably soft, and fell asleep instead of watching the time. The moon was high when he roused Aly.

It did not take long to saddle the stallion. Very soon Aly was picking his way down the wadi, and thence out into the desert. Once clear of the oasis, he let the horse have its head.

The desert was a silver landscape reaching to the star-spangled horizon. It was so light that Aly could see the tracks left by the others, but he did not follow them closely, for he knew in which direction they were going. There was only one way to the Tunisian border, east across the Chott Melhrir, to Tozeur. Many times he had heard his brother talk of this route. It was the shortest, and it avoided all large villages.

Yusuf was somewhere in front with the others from Yelten. Aly knew he must not let his brother see him, for Yusuf would try to prevent him going on alone.

Okba enjoyed the coolness of the night, and maintained a steady gallop. Only where there was loose, deep sand, did he drop to a trot.

There was a good deal of firm going, and when they came to the Chott Melhrir it was like being on a race-course. The surface was ideal for galloping.

Aly loosened the reins, and the stallion leaped forward. The air whistled round the boy's ears as he lay forward on Okba's neck, and tried to whip the turban from his head. The stallion's hoofs made no sound on the friable surface. Around them the desert was equally silent. Not even the cry of a jackal could be heard. The world seemed unreal. Only they were alive.

He thought of Mamounah. How was she standing up to the journey? Had she managed to cling onto the horse which she shared with two others?

The heavy droning of an airplane bound for the Congo disturbed the silence and made him look up. He could see the wing-tip lights only faintly against the immensity of the sky. The plane was doing over five hundred miles an hour, but it seemed scarcely to move.

Passengers up there would be eating and drinking, or blissfully sleeping, unaware of the tragedies that occurred below them in the desert. In a few hours they would span the Sahara, something which took camels three months to do.

Aly was moving much faster than a camel. Okba was eating up the length of the *chott*, travelling so rapidly that Aly was confident he would overtake the others before daylight. He wondered if the deserters would halt for a rest before dawn. The horses could not keep going indefinitely.

When after several hours Okba twitched his ears to the right, Aly knew that someone was near. He slowed to a trot, and warily changed direction.

Before long he saw camels and horses on the near side of a ridge, and knew that it was Yusuf's party. Why had they stopped?

He dismounted and led Okba along the bottom of a gully. He got close enough to see that men were lying down on the ridge, watching something beyond. They spoke in low voices.

Aly wanted his brother beside him, but was afraid to call out. There were some among the men who would want to take Okba from him and send him back to Yelten.

"I will not lose you again," he whispered to the stallion. "We go on together."

He moved round to the left, well clear of the ridge, for he wanted to see what interested the others.

From behind a sand dune he looked down into a dry gorge which had once contained a roaring torrent. There was no water now, but at the far end was a camp fire. Hummel and his men had paused to cook a meal, and to rest the horses.

Aly grunted with satisfaction, and went still farther to

the left before mounting and making a detour to get level with the camp. There were clumps of the grey-green shrub which was so popular with camels. He tethered Okba to one of these bushes, and crawled towards the fire.

The horses were bunched together, and beside them was the towering shape of Polskie, who always seemed to be left on guard while the others fed and rested.

On either side were grouped the women and children. They were passing round a waterskin from which they were drinking, but they had been given no food. The children had cried themselves to sleep; the women were too exhausted to talk.

Aly worked his way round the horses, and heard the sergeant talking angrily and harshly. The others still feared and obeyed him.

Wriggling on his stomach, Aly got within ten yards of the hostages. He tried to pick out his sister, but one huddled figure was much like another.

Then he noticed something moving slowly towards him from the left. At first he thought it was a slinking jackal, but soon saw that it was a man in a shirt and short, baggy trousers. The man was heading for the boulder behind which Aly lay.

He moistened his lips, and reached for the revolver which was tucked in his belt. He did not want to have to use it, but the feel of it gave him courage.

He remained motionless and watched the other's stealthy approach.

11 Rescued!

He soon saw that it was not one of the deserters. It was an Arab, but he was not certain that it was one of those from Yelten. It could be a wandering nomad attracted by the fire.

The man wormed his way nearer, rarely lifting his face more than a few inches from the ground. Then, when no more than a dozen yards separated them, Aly recognized his brother. As he had been crawling, his usual limp had not identified him.

He put away the gun, and glanced towards the men at the fire. They were listening to Franz Hummel.

Aly risked showing himself to one side of the boulder, and hissed: "Yusuf!"

His brother dropped flat, and remained still for several seconds. Then he raised his head, and Aly beckoned. Yusuf crawled over and lay beside him.

"How did you get here? Who is with you?" he asked.

"I am alone, and have Okba. I was trying to find Mamounah."

Yusuf hid his surprise, and studied the group of women and children.

"She is the nearest one lying down," he whispered. "I recognize the bangle on her ankle. She seems unharmed."

"Allah be praised!" said Aly, fervently. "Shall I call to her? The men will not hear me."

"No, the other women will raise an outcry, and we shall be betrayed. We must attract her attention without alarming the others."

Aly picked up some small stones, and began to toss them towards his sister, who was either sleeping or resting with closed eyes. The first two stones missed her, but made no sound as they fell on the soft sand. The third struck her lightly on the leg, and she sat up, looking about her.

Another swift glance to make sure neither of the men was looking in his direction, and Aly put out a hand and waved it up and down to attract her attention. Then he crooked his finger.

It was a risk, but he relied on the fact that Mamounah was very quick witted. She lay down again, and began to inch herself along the ground in their direction. Not only had she to avoid being seen by her captors, but her companions must not see what she was doing.

She moved slowly. Sometimes she remained motionless for a full minute. The poor light helped her. The moon was setting, and it would be soon dark.

A movement at the camp fire alarmed them. Someone had risen to his feet, and Aly feared that the party was about to move off. But it was only one of the men going to relieve the Pole with the horses, so that he could come in and have his share of the food.

Mamounah was now only a few feet from the boulder, and her luck still held. The other women were too exhausted to notice what she was doing.

A final lift from her elbows, and she rolled into the shadow of the rock, alongside Aly. She did not speak, but her big eyes questioned them as she looked from one to the other.

"Are you hurt?" whispered Yusuf.

She shook her head, too frightened to speak.

"Then come—!" said Yusuf. "We will creep away and join the others."

Aly turned so that his mouth was close to his brother's ear. He had made a firm resolve.

"Take her back, Yusuf, and tell the others to be ready to pick up their women folk. I am going to try and give them the chance to do so."

"There is nothing you can do," began Yusuf. "These men will shoot you. What can you do against so many?"

"I will do my best," Aly whispered back. "Someone must try. Go quickly, before Mamounah is missed. I shall be safe for I have Okba."

Yusuf looked at him wonderingly. He did not understand the change in his brother. Ever since he had come into possession of the stallion, he had assumed a new stature, and new confidence.

The moon had finally dipped. The stars were dimming. Yusuf knew they must take advantage of the darkness before dawn.

He squeezed Aly's elbow, and hissed: "I will take her back, and we will be ready for anything that may happen. Be careful!"

He nudged Mamounah, and they crawled towards the ridge, vanishing from sight almost immediately.

Aly did not wait. Any moment now he expected Mamounah's absence to be noticed. Or Sergeant Hummel might give the order for the march to re-commence.

He circled around the resting women and children, and made for the horses, which were huddled together in the care of a single man. Now that the moon was down, he could move more freely.

Soon he was close enough to see that the horses were only lightly tethered. In some cases their reins had been dropped over their heads and hung to the ground. The deserters relied on fatigue keeping the animals still. The man in charge sometimes walked around them, puffing at one of the cigarettes which had been brought from Yelten

Satisfied, Aly went back to Okba, who tossed his head

and stamped impatiently. Aly mounted, and rode quietly to the farther side of the grouped horses.

The vital moment had come. He drew the revolver from his belt and pushed off the safety-catch. Then he kicked in his heels and sent Okba straight for the other horses, at the same time firing over their heads.

The effect was instantaneous. The men by the fire leaped to their feet, grabbing for their weapons. The man guarding the horses swung about and saw an indistinct shape bearing down on him out of the darkness. As he opened his mouth to shout, a bullet whistled past his ear, and he dropped flat to the sand.

The shouts, the shots, and sight of Okba galloping towards them, alarmed the other animals. They spun around, jerking their reins loose from the bushes, rapidly becoming a frenzied, stampeding mob, bumping into each other, tripping over trailing reins, shrilling with fright.

Aly fired the remaining shots into the air. The horses scattered, while Okba galloped straight ahead. Aly wanted to get out of range before the shooting started.

His move had been so unexpected that he was almost clear before guns blazed. He could hear bullets whining overhead, or thudding into the sand.

To add to the confusion, he yelled at the top of his voice, still further panicking the horses. One got a foot in a rein and fell heavily, but the sand was deep, and it was up in a moment, straining to catch up with the others.

When he had chased them about two miles, he was satisfied, and slowed to look back.

Most of Hummel's men had gone after their mounts, but the sergeant had stopped behind. He was bellowing for them to return, and there was fear in his voice. He did not know if they were about to be attacked by Arabs in force. He could not know that Aly was alone.

The boy rode towards the ridge behind which the men from Yelten were screened. Now was their chance to dash in and collect the hostages. He wondered if they were doing this. He heard no sound.

Then he saw other figures running for the ridge. Someone had crept in and told the hostages to make a dash for it. They were making for the waiting camels and horses.

He sighed with satisfaction. This part of his plan had worked well. By the time the deserters discovered what had happened, it would be too late. They could not take up the pursuit of the hostages without their horses.

He saw Mamounah hanging on behind Yusuf, who was riding a horse that was mostly skin and bone. He was ashamed to be so much better mounted, but he still had a great deal to do, and would need all Okba's speed and endurance.

"Come with us!" called Yusuf, who had recognized the white stallion in the gloom. "You have done all you wished to do, Aly. Mamounah is safe."

"I am going to try and recover the Caid's treasure," shouted Aly. "Go swiftly with Mamounah, and Allah be with you!"

He turned away before his brother could say more. A lone horseman was galloping towards him. Someone had caught a laggard horse.

Aly pulled up, and awkwardly reloaded the revolver, dropping several cartridges in the process. As the man drew nearer, Aly opened fire. He did not expect to score a hit, but wanted to draw attention to himself, and prevent the rider going after the hostages.

The man shouted angrily, and turned, firing with an automatic rifle. His mount, not accustomed to firearms being discharged past its ears, promptly reared. Not expecting this, and being impeded by his rifle, the German fell off. Before he could scramble up the horse had vanished into the darkness.

Aly rode away grinning; he knew that his friends would get clear.

Dawn was not far away, and although he wanted to remain in the vicinity, he did not want to be seen. He rode into a hollow which he had noticed previously, and dismounted, rolling a small boulder onto Okba's reins to hold the stallion. Then he crawled back up the slope to keep watch.

There was a pink glow in the eastern sky. Streaks of green and gold appeared above the dunes. Slowly these brightened and spread, then the red rim of the sun appeared, peeping to make sure that the world was ready for another day to begin.

Aly never tired of watching the sun rise. When it came clear of the horizon it was a glowing golden ball, growing more dazzling every moment, so that he was obliged to turn his eyes away because of the hurt from it.

Daylight was racing across the desert, brushing aside the thin veil of mist which had collected in the hollows, until every detail of the landscape for endless miles was clear. The cool of the night went with the darkness. The temperature was rapidly rising.

Aly looked the other way, towards the eight angry men who were trying to recapture the horses. Some of them were visible, others were hidden behind the rolling dunes.

The trailing reins slowed some of the runaways enough for the more fleet-footed men to come up with them. Two were caught and mounted, and used to ride down others. When nine had been secured, no attempt was made to round up any more. The deserters had a horse apiece, and a spare one to carry the precious waterskins.

All this took time. The sun was high, and the men were hot and weary by the time they were ready to move off towards the Tunisian border. They vented their tempers on their mounts. By that time the hostages were out of sight, and no attempt was made to follow them. Henceforth the deserters would have no living screen to hide them if they were spotted from the air, but they were still in the stolen Arab robes, and from a distance they looked like nomads.

Aly was determined to try and recover the Caid's treasure. Neither did he like the idea of these men escaping.

"The Caid would have tried to stop them," he reasoned, "but he is ill and far away. Only Okba and I are left."

By this time air patrols would be seeking the runaways. He looked hopefully to the north, but the sky was clear. The eight men had lashed and kicked the horses to a floundering gallop. Aly was sad to see Okba's stable companions treated so harshly.

He watched them go, not daring to leave cover until they were out of sight, but he did not intend to let them get too far ahead. They still had forty miles to go to the border, and the horses would not last that distance unless they were rested, fed, and given water. There was also a distinct chance that they might lose their way, for there was no marked trail.

Then, as he watched them, a lone Arab on a camel appeared over a ridge ahead. Seeing what he imagined to be a party of nomads, he turned in their direction, speeding up his camel.

The deserters galloped towards him, and he realized too late that there was something odd about them. He turned, and tried to get away, beating his camel into a lumbering, awkward trot.

One of the leading riders stopped and raised a rifle. The camel folded up, and pitched its rider into the sand.

Aly watched the deserters haul him to his feet. In the clear morning light he saw them heap blows on the man. They were demanding something of him, and Aly guessed they were ordering him to lead them to the nearest water supply.

Finally the Arab was lifted onto the horse in front of Franz Hummel, and the party moved off again, slightly changing direction. The man had agreed to lead them to water.

Aly waited until they had passed over the next ridge, then rode out of the hollow. He now had a double reason for following them. His own water supply was very low, and he knew that Okba, like the horses in front, needed a drink.

12 The Underground Reservoir

Aly knew nothing of the country ahead. He had never been so far to the east. From his brother he knew that there were no towns or villages of importance before the border. He knew there must be some waterholes, otherwise the merchants from Tunisia would not have come that way. He felt sure the captured Arab must know of some such place. He followed as closely as he dared.

The sun beat down with an intensity which would have terrified anyone unaccustomed to the Sahara, but Aly had spent his life in the desert, and accepted the blistering heat as a matter of course.

He was careful not to be seen by those in front, for he guessed they would be looking back frequently to see if they were being pursued. He contrived to keep high ground between them all the time.

For an hour he followed through a region of stones and deep sand. There were few high dunes, and no vegetation. Those in front were not travelling fast, but their horses must have suffered considerably.

He had dismounted for about the sixth time, to peer over a ridge to find out how far they were ahead, when he saw that the party was approaching some ruins perched on the edge of what appeared to be a deep wadi. They were very extensive ruins. He could see stretches of massive walls, and the remains of several towers. He did not know that they were a reminder of the Roman occupation of North Africa in the first century. Here there had once stood a big, permanent encampment of the Third Legion, which served the Emperor Trajan. It had been an important fortress, with everything necessary to make life possible for a garrison in those days.

Aly knew nothing of this. He lay in the blistering sun and watched the horsemen pass through an archway.

"Here there must be water!" he told the stallion. "Before we go any farther we will share what I have left."

The water in the goat skin was warm and brackish, but there was sufficient to slake his thirst and to let Okba wash the dust from his throat. He spent some minutes wiping the sand from the horse's nostrils and eyes. Okba stood placidly, grateful for these attentions.

The wadi curved to the west, and Aly saw that by riding along the bottom he could get close to the ruins unseen. He hugged the near-side cliff, and finally saw one of the towers above him. In the time of the Romans that tower had stood on the bank of a considerable river, but now the river bed was dry.

He saw a way up the cliff. At one point it overhung, and he led the horse into the shade, loosened the girths, and removed bit and bridle.

He slung the goat skin across his back, made sure he had the revolver, and began to climb. A few minutes later he was peering cautiously over the top.

Ahead of him was a flat, square area, about sixty yards across. It had been a forum, or maybe a parade-ground, and was paved with flat slabs of stone now covered by sand. It was surrounded by a thick sandstone wall in which there were several openings. He ducked down when he heard voices beyond one of the former gateways.

The harsh voice of Sergeant Hummel was mingled with the shrill, frightened tones of the Arab.

Aly watched, keeping low. Hummel was making for a small, arched opening in the far corner of the square. He held a rope, and the other end of this was tied to the Arab's wrists. He was an old man, bearded, with a pronounced limp. Hummel was prodding him forward with his revolver. Four of the other Germans tailed behind, laden with empty waterskins.

"If there is no water—you die!" the sergeant was telling his captive.

"It is here, Sidi, I swear, but far below!" the old man assured him. "When the river disappeared long, long ago, the Ancients dug tunnels to find it. There are many steps down to the water, and my old legs will not carry me."

"They will!" growled Hummel, grimly.

They paused in the opening, which was at the top of a steep flight of steps. Hummel and some of the others produced torches and shone them inside. The sergeant grunted, and a man with a torch disappeared down the steps.

The rest waited impatiently. They were gaunt and bleary-eyed, and their Arab robes only partially hid their ragged uniforms. Their comrades had been left with the horses beyond the outer wall. It was a long time before the man shouted up from below. Hummel bellowed back, and they all entered the opening, forcing the old Arab ahead of them despite his protests.

Minutes passed, and Aly waited. There was still the chance of being seen by those with the horses, but they were not in sight. They would be keeping in the shade of the wall.

He finally crawled over the edge of the cliff and made for one of the side walls. He had left his sandals with the horse, and moved silently towards the top of the steps.

He flattened himself in the opening and looked down the steep flight. It was cooler in there, and he could smell the water below. It would be a subterranean stream. He had seen such places before. They were sometimes linked by man-made tunnels centuries old.

The water beneath these ruins was not used for irrigation, for the place was uninhabited. Only casual travellers, knowing of the water supply, would pause there for a night.

Voices came faintly to his ears; the steps went down for a considerable distance. It would be no easy task bringing up sufficient water for all those horses.

He started to creep down the steps, finding that they curved midway. When he had turned this bend he could see a light below. He judged it was another hundred feet below him.

Someone was already returning, carrying a filled waterskin. Aly could hear it gurgling.

There was a narrow niche in the rock beside him, and he squeezed back into this. Now a second man commenced to climb. He called out to the first climber, who answered breathlessly. They continued upwards in silence. They needed no light, for there was only one way to the top. When they turned the bend they would see daylight.

Aly turned his face to the wall to lessen the chance of being seen, and held his breath. Both men were panting noisily as they passed him. They each had a heavy load of waterskins.

They reached the top, but he remained where he was, for he could hear others coming up. In the rear came Sergeant Hummel, and he flashed his torch on and off.

Aly feared that he might switch it on as he came around the bend, but he dared not leave his hiding place. He could only squeeze himself back as far as possible and hope for the best.

Hummel was urging the others on with scathing remarks, but by the time he reached the bend he was breathless enough to be silent. He lurched against the rock and almost brushed Aly's back, but he had now switched off the torch.

Aly relaxed. The way was clear for him to go down and fill his own waterskin. He wondered what had happened to the Arab. They had not brought him up with them.

He went down the steps in total darkness. He had only a few matches left, and he wanted to save these until he was at the bottom. The steps were worn and uneven, but he was barefooted and felt each step with his toes, one hand on the wall to steady himself.

It got colder as he descended, and the darkness could be almost felt. No sound came from the depths.

Finally there were no more steps. His foot found level rock. He put out his hands in sweeping gestures, but felt nothing. He had reached a large chamber, or cave, and he ventured to strike one of the precious matches.

As he did so there came the sound of a low groan from the left. It startled him so much that he staggered back against the bottom step, and sat down heavily. The match flared in his fingers.

A gasp escaped him. Only a yard ahead of him was the edge of a pool of black water. The ledge on which he had descended was only four feet wide. If he had gone forward another step he would have been in the water.

A few paces to his left the Arab lay in a huddled heap, his feet protruding over the sinister pool. He stirred as Aly moved towards him, and tried to sit up.

"Don't move!" warned Aly, for he feared that the dazed man would slip in. "I am a friend."

The match burned his fingers, and he dropped the glowing end. The injured man gasped, and Aly squatted beside him in the darkness, taking hold of his ragged robe.

"I saw you meet those foreigners," he explained. "Have they hurt you?"

"They forced me to come down here with them. I fell at the bottom, and the sergeant kicked me in the head. I must have become unconscious. Where are they now, and who are you?"

As briefly as possible Aly told him what had been happening, that the deserters were now watering their horses, and that he was alone and badly in need of water for himself and Okba.

The old man said that his name was Keliba, and that he was a wandering marabout, or holy man. He had come from Tozeur, and was trying to make his way to the villages at the foot of the Aurès Mountains. He had rested for some days in these ruins, and had only left that morning. The place was called Bulla.

"They will be coming back for more water," Aly told him. "Is there anywhere to hide down here?"

By this time Keliba had shakily gained his feet, keeping well back against the wall. He said that during his stay he had explored part of this subterranean world. They were now inside a huge storage reservoir which the Romans had hewn out of the solid rock. The original river ran beneath the wadi, and was linked with the reservoir by an ancient culvert. It might be possible to hide in that.

Aly lit another match, and they cautiously edged their way to the left. Almost immediately they heard voices on the steps. Men were coming down for more water.

The mouth of the culvert was at the end of the pool. The water was no more than three feet deep, and there was only a slight inflow from the hidden stream.

Waist deep, they groped their way inside the culvert as a light reached the bottom of the steps. Three men had arrived. Polskie was one of them, and he carried four waterskins.

When these three men reached the ledge at the edge of

the pool, they began to exclaim excitedly, stabbing the darkness with the beams of their torches.

"What do they say?" whispered the old Arab.

"I do not understand them, for they are not speaking French, but they have missed you. We had better go farther back, for they will search."

They groped their way forward in complete darkness, for they dared not show a light. Aly, who was in the lead, had no idea how deep the water would be. Keliba hung onto his shoulders, and followed step by step.

The water crept up beyond Aly's chest. They paused, leaning against the side of the culvert, looking back nervously. Someone shone a torch into the entrance, and shouted to the others.

The marabout's teeth began to chatter, for the water was icy cold, yet up above the temperature would be over one hundred degrees in the shade.

The three men soon gave up the search. They had decided that the injured Arab had rolled into the pool and drowned.

The roof of the culvert was only two feet above Aly's head, but when a little later he explored farther with the aid of a match he discovered that the river ran through a natural tunnel so lofty that the feeble light did not show the top of it.

The river was wide and shallow. Rocks protruded in several places, and they waded to one and climbed on top. The marabout had some dates, and they shared these.

The river came from the mountains in the north, and flowed south to lose itself in the heart of the Sahara. When the snow melted on the mountain peaks there would be a great flow of water, but now it was scarcely a foot deep.

They sat there shivering, talking in low voices, and wondering how long these men would remain at Bulla. As both men and horses were exhausted, Aly believed they would stay long enough to recover their strength. They had brought ample supplies of food from Yelten. Inside the ruins they would be safe from observation from the air. Their only danger would come from travellers heading westwards from Tozeur.

"Not many use this route at this time of the year," said Keliba. "It is cooler nearer the mountains. I only came this way because I wished to visit the tomb of Sidi Marhaba, which is beyond Ain Zara."

Aly knew that was the tomb where he had found shelter from the sandstorm and had first encountered the deserters. He marvelled that the old man could make such journeys across the desert alone.

Several times he went to the mouth of the culvert to see if the deserters had left, but it proved necessary for them to make three journeys to the pool before they had sufficient water for their horses. Only then did they settle down above, and Aly decided that it was safe to return to the steps.

The marabout was cold and exhausted. Aly gave him his own robe as an extra covering, and made him as comfortable as he could before telling him to sleep.

"They will not come here again until they need more water," he said. "I must go to my horse."

Keliba grunted, already half asleep. In darkness Aly filled the waterskin and cautiously climbed to the top.

There was no sign of movement. Tracks in the sand told him where they had gone, and presently he was peering into the outer courtyard where they slept in the shade of a massive wall. The horses were tethered nearby, heads drooping, tails switching to keep away the flies. They were no longer thirsty, but they were very hungry. A hollowed-out stone had been used as a trough for them to drink. Possibly it had been used by the Romans for the same purpose two thousand years earlier.

Sergeant Hummel was snoring loudly, and Aly was tempted to crawl over to him to seek the Caid's jewels. He had almost decided to do this when he thought to count the sleepers.

There were only seven. Where was the eighth man?

Something made him glance upwards, and there on top of the nearest tower the big Pole stood silhouetted against the brassy sky. He was staring to the north. His back was turned, but if he had looked round he would have seen Aly.

Aly hurriedly ducked under the archway, and crossed the square to the wadi, into which he descended with his heavy load of water.

Okba heard him coming and turned his head, but he was not alone. Something stirred on the ground beside him, there was a piteous whining, and a bedraggled figure crawled to Aly.

He stared unbelievingly. Plastered with sand, scarcely able to stand, with bloodshot eyes and gaping mouth, was the saluki.

"Fellah!" Aly dropped to his knees. "How did you come here?"

The dog licked his hand; its tongue was like black leather. It was parched with thirst.

The first thing was to pour some water down Fellah's throat. The dog gulped gratefully, lying on its side. Its paws were raw. It had come many, many miles. Aly could only guess what had happened.

When Mamounah and her mother had taken refuge with the others, Fellah had tried to find Aly. Failing, he had hunted around the oasis and had come upon the trail left by Okba when he had been turned loose by Selim. Fellah had followed this into the desert, believing that Aly was riding the horse. He had never caught up with Okba, but had trailed him back to the oasis for the second time, too late to start out with Aly.

Grimly he had picked up the new trail, and had been travelling ever since, still seeking them. Finally he had come to the wadi where the stallion was tethered under the overhanging cliff. There his strength had failed.

Now Fellah was contented, and slept, while Aly gave the rest of the water to Okba. Then, almost as weary as his dog, Aly stretched out beside them and also slept.

13 The Gun-Runners

A loud noise roused Aly, and he rubbed his eyes, not understanding where he was until he saw Okba on one side of him and the saluki sleeping on the other. Then he remembered, and scrambled to his feet.

The sun had set, and already the bottom of the wadi was in deep shadow. He ran from under the overhang of the cliff, and saw a helicopter passing low over the ruins. It was the sound of its motor which had awakened him.

Twice it circled the ancient fort, and he knew it had been sent to locate the deserters. They would have heard it coming and hidden themselves.

Aly shouted and waved his arms, but the airmen could not see him in the wadi. He was unable to attract their attention, and a few minutes later saw them turn away to the north. They wished to be back at their base before nightfall.

He was tight-lipped with disappointment when he returned to his companions. Fellah raised his head and feebly wagged his tail, but he was still weak.

"We need food," muttered Aly, "and I do not know how to get it. These foreigners have some, but they guard it well."

He could have slept longer, but now that darkness was near there was much for him to do. He had to fetch the old marabout, and refill the waterskin. He had to watch the movements of the deserters, and he had to try and get food.

"I must leave you for a while," he told the animals. "Rest, Fellah, and get strong again. I will try and get something for you to eat."

He made his way to the spot where he could climb the side of the wadi. The moon had not yet risen.

As soon as he reached the top he heard loud voices coming from the inner section of the ruins. There was a quarrel in progress. He crept along the shadowed walls until he could see what was happening.

Sergeant Hummel had his back to a stone pillar, and six men were angrily crowding in on him, shaking their fists and shouting. He had a gun in his hand, and was hoarse with anger. The Pole was up on the watch-tower, taking no part in the dispute.

By sheer force of personality Hummel at last dominated the others. They were afraid of him. Aly could not tell what the quarrel was about, but he saw they had left their remaining food supplies and waterskins close to where the horses were tethered.

Keeping in the darkest shadows, he crawled forward, ready to turn and run if anyone looked round. They were now listening to Hummel, who was speaking in a more reasonable tone.

Aly squirmed the last few yards and gripped one corner of a partially filled sack. He felt dates inside, and began to back away, towing his prize with him.

When he reached the cover of the archway, he rose to his feet, lifted the sack onto his shoulder, and ran with it to the edge of the cliff, where he deposited it behind a boulder. He still had to go underground for the marabout.

Again he groped his way down that long, dark flight of steps. He had three matches left, but did not strike one until he reached the bottom, where he called softly: "Keliba, it is Aly! Where are you?"

The old man was awake, very cold, and very frightened, for he feared that he had been abandoned. Aly pulled him towards the steps before he could ask questions.

"We must leave here as soon as I can fill the waterskin," he urged. "Hurry!"

It was a slow business getting Keliba up the steps. They had to stop many times for him to rest, and Aly feared that someone would come down from above. Nobody appeared by the time they reached the top, and after making sure that the open square was empty, he hurried his companion to where he had left the dates.

Keliba wanted to eat some at once, but Aly said they would feed when they reached the animals, and not before. Carrying both the dates and the waterskin, he had a hard task getting the old man down the cliff. It was a great relief when Fellah limped to meet him.

The marabout was on the verge of exhaustion, but recovered when given water and a double handful of dates. Aly tipped out a pile in front of the stallion, and stoned some for Fellah.

Okba attacked the dates with gusto, chewing the flesh from the stones, and dropping the latter from the corner of his mouth. He loved dates, but Fellah, although ravenous, turned from them in disgust. It took a lot of coaxing to get him to swallow any.

It was a simple meal, but dates are very nourishing. A man could exist on a handful a day, and the heap which Okba had devoured would sustain him until something better could be found.

By this time the moon was up, and the desert around brightly lit. As he ate his frugal supper, Aly did some hard thinking.

At last he said: "The helicopter may pass this way again tomorrow. I will make a sign that the airmen will see."

He explained his idea to Keliba, who agreed that it was

a good idea, although it would be a waste of time if the deserters left before dawn.

"I do not think they will go tonight," said Aly. "Their horses have not rested enough. The sergeant knows that. If they are wise they will stay here until tomorrow night. By that time the search will have gone in other directions. So now I will go and make my sign."

Fellah would have gone with him despite his sore paws, but Aly made him stay with the others.

This time he climbed the other side of the wadi, and found himself on a flat, sandy expanse that was dotted with large stones. He had noted this the previous morning. It was directly opposite the ruins, and when he looked back he could see the lookout on the tower.

He moved farther away until he was certain he was not visible to this man, then set to work to gather large, white stones which he proceeded to lay out in the form of a large cross.

It was hard work, and his back ached from stooping and lifting long before he had finished. By then he had made a cross of stones more than twenty feet long and nearly as wide.

He hoped that in daylight it might attract the attention of any passing airman, whether in helicopter or spotter plane. It would be recognized as a signal, and would cause closer investigation of the ruins to be made. If the hidden men opened fire, the plane would radio to the nearest patrols.

He felt very satisfied with himself as he straightened up and pushed back his turban; then a sound coming from the east made him turn round.

He had heard the angry bellowing of a camel.

At first he could see nothing, but when he stooped low and looked along the moonlit ground, he could see shapes moving slowly in his direction. There were at least a score of men and camels.

"Merchants from Tozeur!" was his instant thought. "They know of the water under the old fort, and are coming to get supplies."

He felt pleased that he would be no longer alone, then realized that the newcomers were in dire danger. They would stumble on the hidden deserters, who would not hesitate to shoot them down.

Merchants were rarely armed these days. They would stand no chance against the well-armed deserters.

"They must be warned," he decided, and set off running in the moonlight to intercept them before they were seen by the watcher on the tower.

As he drew nearer he saw that some of the men marched on foot beside the heavily laden camels, while three others were mounted on horses. This was unusual. Traders did not ride horses in the desert, for it meant carrying extra water.

"Peace be with you!" he shouted. "Come no farther!"

The leading horseman raised a hand above his head. The line of camels halted. The man rode towards Aly.

"Who are you, and whence do you come?" he demanded, without returning the conventional greeting.

He was a tall, dark-bearded man in semi-European clothing, although he wore a turban and a short cloak. The moonlight showed that he had a gun belt, with a revolver at his side. Across the high pommel of his saddle was a modern rifle.

"I am Aly ben Rabah, and I am from Yelten, where I am in the employ of the Caid Sidi Ramdan ben Mizan," replied Aly, not without pride. "I come to warn you of danger—there!"

He pointed towards the ruins.

By this time another horseman, and three men on foot, had come forward and now surrounded him. He was surprised to see that they were all heavily armed. There was something unusually grim and purposeful about them.

"What is this danger?" growled the bearded leader.

"There are eight runaways from the Legion of foreigners, and they have many guns. If you go nearer they will shoot you down and take what they want from you, for they are trying to escape into Tunisia."

The bearded man frowned and muttered something to the others, who did not look at all frightened.

"Tell us more about these foreigners, boy!" he ordered curtly. "How did they come here? Why are you here, and who is with you?"

Aly resented his tone. He had run all the way to do these men a good turn, and they were treating him with contempt. He told them about the deserters, from his first contact with them until the present time. He told how they had come to Yelten and carried off hostages, and how these had been rescued. He told how he had been following and watching these men, but did not mention that he hoped to recover the treasure which they had taken from the Caid's house.

The bearded man's frown grew fiercer, and he barked many questions. During this time the camels had slowly approached, and Aly noticed that their loads were unusual. They were not carrying produce, but long wooden cases wrapped in canvas. Only two of them were laden with food and water.

Suddenly the leader growled: "Seize him, and tie him!"

Before Aly could run, two of the men had grabbed him and twisted his arms behind his back. Although he kicked and struggled, his gun was taken from him, his wrists were tied together, and he finished up sprawling on the sand, looking up angrily at his attackers as he shouted: "I came here to warn you, and you treat me like this! Why have you done this to me?"

"We trust no one," growled the bearded horseman. "It is true that you warned us about these foreigners, but it is better that you are kept safely until we have dealt with them. In due course you will be freed."

"But you cannot fight these men!" protested Aly. "They are soldiers—trained to battle—and ruthless. You would have no chance. Go some other way, and do not let them see you."

One of the men lifted him to his feet.

"Be quiet! You talk too much. Hussein Ali knows what he is doing. We also are trained to battle. We need to shelter in that old fort, and a few runaway soldiers are not going to stop us."

Aly's jaw sagged, and he looked at the canvas-covered cases with new understanding.

He knew the name of Hussein Ali. There was a big reward offered for his capture, for he was a rebel against the French, and one of the leaders of the resistance movement who specialized in gun-running from Tunisia. The camels were laden with cases of rifles and ammunition. This was gun-running on a large scale.

Hussein Ali travelled by night only. He used this southern route from the border, and the ruined fort was one of his regular stopping places. He renewed his water supplies there, and rested men and camels.

The camels had been made to kneel, and Aly was told to stay with them.

"If you try to shout and warn the foreigners, I shall cut your throat!" the man in charge of him said amiably.

Aly's thoughts were in a turmoil. Why should he want to warn the foreigners? They were men of violence, and they had done his people nothing but harm. He had no wish to warn them, but man for man he was sure they were more than a match for these gun-runners.

He did not voice his opinions. It would be wise to keep silent and see if the situation could not be turned to his advantage. He was glad he had not told his captors about the marabout or about Okba. Keliba was unlikely to come looking for him.

Hussein Ali dismounted and went forward on foot with half a dozen of his men. The other two remained with Aly and the camels.

The moon was bright, but within a minute of leaving the others Hussein Ali and his companions vanished from sight. Unless the man on top of the tower was very keen sighted, he would not see them approach.

If they could get across the wadi unnoticed, they would be able to creep into the ruins and make a surprise attack. That was their plan, and the men with Aly were confident that it would succeed.

They sat on either side of him and talked freely of their journeys across the border. They had made this trip many times. There were rebel sympathizers in Tunisia who supplied them with guns. It was merely a matter of getting them past the frontier patrols.

One of the men had been to Yelten, and knew about the Caid Sidi Ramdan ben Mizan. He said that the Caid was stupid not to secretly join the rebels, for the time would come when he would either have to do so or be destroyed. Aly still said nothing.

Half an hour passed, and the men no longer talked. They were staring towards the ruins, and straining their ears. It was time that something happened.

Aly began to wonder if there was any chance that the gun-runners could get the better of the deserters. If they did this they would find the Caid's jewels. They would be sold for the rebel funds, perhaps used to purchase more rifles!

He was turning this idea over in his mind when from the distance came the sound of a single shot, followed by the splutter of an automatic rifle. Then came a wild fusillade from many weapons, and a vivid flash which could have been made only by a hand grenade.

The deserters had not been taken by surprise!

Aly's two companions were on their feet, jabbering excitedly. They were anxious to know what had happened, but they had been ordered not to leave the camels untended.

Time passed. Aly's mouth was parched with excitement when from somewhere in the fading moonlight came a hoarse cry: "Help! Moulai, help!"

"It is Hussein!" gasped one of the men, and they raced towards the spot whence the call for help had come.

Aly got up and wrenched at the cord which tied his wrists. For the moment his captors had forgotten him. Their leader was in trouble.

When the cords would not give, Aly looked about him for something with which to free himself. The kneeling camels gurgled and grunted beside him, chewing methodically, and complaining that their loads had not been removed. The horses drooped their weary heads and took comfort in being close together.

Nowhere could he see a knife, or anything with a sharp edge.

Voices were coming nearer. Dimly he could make out the two men slowly returning. Between them they supported Hussein Ali. He had been wounded. No one else was with him.

It was time to go. Although his arms were tied, Aly's legs were free. He began to run to the right, intending to circle around the three gun-runners and get back to Keliba, Okba, and Fellah.

14 The Man they Left Behind

When he was a safe distance away, Aly paused and looked back. The gun-runners had got their leader onto a horse, and had mounted the others. The three of them turned and rode towards the east, abandoning the camels.

Nothing could have told Aly more clearly that complete disaster had overtaken the attackers. They had been shot down by the deserters, and only Hussein Ali had escaped. Now he was abandoning everything to save his own skin.

Aly heard men coming from the other direction. In the failing moonlight he saw six or seven of the deserters emerging from the wadi and making for the camels. They were eager to see what loot had fallen into their hands.

He crouched behind a boulder and let them pass. They were in high spirits. Apparently they had seen the Arabs creeping up on them, and had let them get close before opening fire. Their harsh laughter made Aly shiver. Here were men to whom death meant nothing.

He waited until they reached the camels, then hurried on his way, stumbling and sometimes falling because of his bound hands. By the time he reached the wadi the moon was setting, and it was much darker.

The descent to the old river bed was not easy with his hands tied behind his back. He slipped and rolled part of the way, but only sustained bruises. Behind him he could hear the camels bellowing and roaring as the men beat them to their feet.

"Fellah!" gasped Aly, a few moments later, when the dog came running towards him with every sign of delight.

Then Keliba called him by name, and came to meet him.

"What has happened, Aly? I feared you were dead. The shooting—!"

"Lower your voice!" hissed Aly, remembering the look-out on the tower. "First free my hands, and I'll tell you what happened."

Back under the overhanging cliff, with Fellah pushing against his legs and Okba nuzzling at his shoulder, he explained the shooting. Keliba had been terrified, but showed no concern at the fate of the gun-runners. He only complained that Aly had not brought him back a camel to ride.

As it would take some time for the deserters to return with the camels, Aly resolved to go up to the fort and see if he could get any more food. With Fellah at his heels, he climbed the cliff path, and almost immediately came upon a dead man sprawled outside the opening in the wall. It was one of the gun-runners who had been badly wounded when the others had been killed. Although riddled with bullets, he had crawled that far before collapsing.

Aly turned away. It would have been better for Hussein Ali if he had heeded the warning to keep away from the ruined fort.

More silent figures lay in the inner courtyard. The look-out on the tower had warned his comrades of their coming and from that moment they had been doomed. There was still someone on the tower; Aly heard him clear his throat.

In the corner where the men had been sleeping was an assortment of waterskins, sacks, garments, and the remains of a meal. He searched for something worth taking away. Fellah found some scraps to his liking and nosed around for more. The camels were still on the farther side of the wadi. Hummel intended getting them under cover before daylight brought another aerial reconnaissance.

Aly discovered some corn bread that the foreigners had found too hard for their teeth, some more dates, and half a sack of carrots, which must have been brought from Yelten by mistake. Everything else had been eaten.

He looked at the horses huddled in the angle of the massive walls. They had been given water, but no food. They were in poor shape, and he did not think they would reach Tunisia. He gave them each a carrot, but retained the rest for Okba.

Whispering for Fellah to follow, he crept out of the ruins with his prizes, and got back to their refuge before the camels had been brought down into the wadi. He told Keliba all he had seen, and again the old man grumbled that Aly had not brought him anything to ride.

"When these men go from here they will leave behind many camels," Aly told him. "You will be able to take your pick. I hope today that my signal will be seen from the air. Meantime, keep watch, for I must get some sleep."

While Keliba chewed bread and dates, and Okba munched contentedly at the carrots, Aly slept with his head pillowed on the saluki.

It was mid-morning when he was wakened by the marabout shaking him. The helicopter had returned, circling low over the desert. The search for the deserters was still proceeding.

Those in the helicopter must have had suspicions about the ruins, for the machine hovered over the tower for some time. The deserters had taken cover, but down in the bottom of the wadi Aly and Keliba were trying to attract attention. They knew they could not be seen by Hummel and his companions.

Evidently they were not sighted by the airmen. The helicopter turned eastward, then someone must have noticed the stone cross which Aly had set out, for the aircraft slowed, circled, and returned.

Aly was frantic with excitement.

"Why do they stay here?" he cried. "Why don't they take back the news, or send it by radio?"

The droning of the aircraft drowned his shouts. The helicopter again passed low over the ruins, from which a volley of shots was suddenly fired. A portion of the rotors flew off, and the machine shuddered. There was an uncanny silence as the motor stopped. The helicopter dropped sideways towards the wadi.

Aly groaned aloud as the deserters turned every gun they possessed on the falling craft. There was a loud crash as it hit the ground no more than fifty yards from the hidden pair. A sheet of flame shot up; the fuel tank had burst.

Aly fancied he saw a figure trying to get out of the cabin, then the flames engulfed everything, and he knew that no one aboard could live.

Horror held him motionless until he realized that Fellah was barking furiously. He turned and grabbed for Okba's bridle.

"Gather up everything!" he ordered Keliba. "We must move from here. They will come to see if anyone still lives. Hasten!"

He silenced the dog, managed to bridle up the stallion, and ran it down the wadi, carrying the saddle with him. The marabout staggered along behind him with the water and the rest of the foodstuff.

They got round the bend in the river bed only just in time. Hummel and some of his companions scrambled down the cliff towards the flaming wreck. They were boasting of their marksmanship.

Aly felt sick at heart, for he felt that he was partially to blame for the deaths of the airmen. If he had not attracted them with his stone cross they would not have come within rifle range of the desperate men who

CP

crouched in the ruins. The question now was whether they had radioed the news before they had been shot down.

The deserters could not approach the blazing helicopter too closely. Aly crept back to listen to them talking, but he understood little, for they spoke in German. Their first elation at their success soon faded. Aly could tell by Hummel's gesture that he was warning them that the non-return of the aircraft to its base could spell disaster. Troops would be sent out to discover what had happened to it. Hummel was urging that they should make an immediate dash for the border.

It was Polskie, the only non-German, who objected to this. His huge figure towered over Hummel as he waved his arms and bellowed. His mild, moon-like face was red with anger. He spluttered in a mixture of German and Polish, and the sergeant's cold insistence only roused the giant Pole to greater fury.

One of the others grabbed at his arm and tried to soothe him, but Polskie threw him off as though he was a rag doll, and the man fell on his back half a dozen paces away.

Polskie was still shouting objections when the man on the ground drew his revolver, and fired.

Nobody expected this, least of all the Pole. The bullet took him in the left arm, and spun him round. He staggered, blinked stupidly, as though he did not understand what had happened, whereupon one of the others jumped up behind him and brought down a rifle butt on his head.

Polskie dropped to his knees, and rolled over, unconscious, his wounded arm bleeding into the sand.

There was uproar. Two of the men turned on the one who had fired the shot, but the sergeant intervened. He calmed them down, and they turned back towards the cliff, leaving the Pole where he lay.

All this time Aly had crouched behind a nearby boulder, half choked by the oily smoke which blew across from the burned-out helicopter. He knew that the sergeant had got his way. They were going to leave immediately.

He went back to where the marabout was holding Fellah.

"They leave!" he said, briefly. "They have gone to fetch the horses."

"And the big one out there—is he dead?" asked Keliba.

"No, he is not dead, but they will leave him behind. He is not one of them. He is not a German."

"Then we will cut his throat?" suggested Keliba with satisfaction.

Aly frowned. He would not let that happen. Remembering how the Pole had been treated by the others, he felt sorry for the man. They had brought him along only because of his great physical strength. He had been useful as a beast of burden, but now they would abandon him.

Before long Hummel and the rest reappeared, crossed the wadi, and rode eastwards. They had laden Polskie's horse with waterskins and the remaining food, and they were in a frantic hurry. The horses had been rested and watered, but they were weak with hunger. Aly again doubted whether they would last to the Tunisian border.

The Pole had not stirred. The others had not given him a glance as they had passed. They were not concerned with his fate.

As soon as they were out of sight Aly ran to the unconscious man, and took the revolver from his belt, transferring it to his own. Keliba, following him, touched his knife.

"Shall I kill the infidel, or will you?" he asked.

"Neither! He may be of use to us. Help me carry him into the shade."

Keliba looked disgusted, but between them they lifted the massive figure out of the sun. There Aly forced some water between his lips, and poured some of it over the man's face to wash away the blood which had trickled from the head wound.

The arm wound was not serious, although it had bled freely. The bullet had only grazed the outside of the upper arm.

Very soon Polskie stirred. He grunted, flung out a hand the size of a dinner plate, and finally opened his amazingly blue eyes, looking up into the gravely intent face of Aly. He muttered something in his own language.

"You are hurt," said Aly, in Arabic, one hand on the revolver. "We will help you."

Polskie frowned and sat up. He closed his eyes for a moment as dizziness overcame him, then opened them to glare about him.

"Where are the others?" he asked, haltingly. "How come you here?"

Like most members of the Foreign Legion, he had been in North Africa long enough to get a rough knowledge of the local language, and Aly laboriously explained to him that Hummel and the rest of the party had ridden for the Tunisian border.

"No!" cried the Pole, and lurched to his feet, swaying like a tree in the wind before pouring out a stream of words which the boy did not understand.

Guessing that he was abusing the others for the way they had treated him, Aly kept silent until he had quietened down. All this while the marabout had remained in the background, and Fellah had crouched not far away, baring his teeth in menacing fashion, for he had not forgotten that this was the man who had once kicked him.

Ignoring his wounds, although they must have given him considerable pain, the Pole suddenly rushed across the wadi and climbed to the top, where he stood glaring after the cloud of dust raised by his late comrades.

When he turned to Aly, who had come up beside him, his expression was no longer puzzled, no longer amiably vacant. His eyes had hardened, and he growled: "They shall pay for this! They treated me like a dog because I was not German, and now they leave me for dead. You have a horse. I shall ride after them and kill them!"

He stopped, for he found himself looking down the barrel of his own gun, which Aly was holding steadily at waist level. "No, I cannot give you my horse, but we will go after them together. I also have business with these men. They ill-treated my people, and they have robbed my Caid. We will deal with them together. They cannot reach the border on those tired horses. We have plenty of time. Do you know for which place they will make?"

The Pole looked at the gun, then at the steady eyes of the speaker. He forced a grin.

"A lion in lamb's clothing!" he exclaimed. "You are right about the horses. They do not expect to reach Tunisia on them. They are making for a place called Oued Zarba. Do you know it? It is owned by a German settler who will hide them until they can be smuggled across the border."

"I do not know of such a place," said Aly, "but the old man may. Come!"

He pointed to Keliba, who was looking up at them from the bottom of the wadi. They went down to him, Aly making the Pole go first, for he was taking no chances.

Keliba said that Oued Zarba was a small settlement where phosphates were mined, about a dozen miles away. It belonged to a German named Von Wagen, who had drilled an artesian well—which made life possible in an otherwise waterless stretch of the desert. He employed about forty men, and his lorries took the phosphate across to Tozeur, in Tunisia. It was probable that the deserters expected to be smuggled over the frontier in this fashion.

Aly's eyes sparkled.

"The horses will get them as far as that. We shall find them there, unless the soldiers reach them first."

Polskie rubbed his big hands together.

"They must not get to them first. You say you have

business with them. Mine is with Franz Hummel. Let me deal with him. That is all I ask."

He would have started at once, but Aly said that it was foolish to travel in the heat, when they could rest now and cover the twelve miles to Oued Zarba in the cool of the night. Besides, he suggested, the Pole's wounds needed attention.

Polskie roared with laughter, saying that his hurts were nothing. The bleeding had stopped. However, he agreed that it would be wiser to wait until the sun went down.

The marabout had gone to choose one of the camels which had been left behind. He intended to continue his interrupted journey as soon as night fell.

Aly and the Pole sat in the shade of the overhanging cliff and listened for airplanes. Aly, who did not altogether trust the big man, kept his distance, the gun ready in his hand, but the Pole made no attempt to cause trouble and seemed content to talk about himself in broken Arabic.

He told of his life in the Legion, and said that he had been forced to join Hummel and the others when they had made their plan to desert. He had not particularly wanted to go, and had been too dull-witted to realize that they only took him with them because of his great strength.

Aly believed him. He felt that Polskie was not naturally a violent man, but that he could be led easily. Yet if he was really roused, as he was now, his wrath would be terrible.

Presently the Pole slept, and Aly was left alone to watch the sky for airplanes which did not come.

In the late afternoon he wakened his companion and sent him to the underground reservoir to fill the water-skins.

Polskie went without a murmur. He was accustomed to taking orders.

15 Polskie Sees Red

The white hills of Oued Zarba showed ahead in the starlight. The phosphate dust covered the desert for half a mile around the mine. It was a desolate spot, without a single tree or bush. Von Wagen, the owner of the concession, had not even troubled to make a garden.

Aly and Polskie were approaching at a walking pace. They had travelled during the early hours of the night, the boy riding, the man walking uncomplainingly beside him. Not once had he suggested sharing the stallion. He was accustomed to slogging many miles on his big feet, and now he was sustained by his desire for vengeance on the men who had once been his comrades.

They had seen the marabout set off towards Zelten before they had left the old fort. He had a strong camel and plenty of water, and he had promised to report the situation to any patrol that he might encounter.

Aly had been disappointed that no such patrol had reached Bulla before they left. Obviously no message had been sent out by radio before the helicopter had crashed.

They had not spoken for more than an hour. Gradually they made out a cluster of buildings at the foot of a low hill, and a larger one nearer the top. A solitary light burned in the latter.

When they were closer they could see a number of shafts running into the hillside, with rails along a rutted track which led towards the distant Tunisian border. A line of stationary trolleys stood on these rails, and there were two lorries on the road beside the track. Everything was plastered with the same white dust.

Aly could not understand why anyone should come to such a place to dig out this white stuff. He could not imagine its being of any value. The Pole had tried to explain the use of phosphates to him, but he was vague about it himself, so Aly was none the wiser.

Yet Von Wagen employed forty Arabs, and made big money. It was one of those things which a true son of the desert, like Aly, could not fathom, and he did not try very hard. He had come there to recover the Caid's jewels, and if he could prevent the deserters escaping before the French patrols came up with them, so much the better.

He dared not ride too near. The horses on which the Germans had arrived would be nearby, and if one of these neighed Okba might reply and betray their presence. It was better to leave the stallion at a safe distance.

There was no real cover, so he tethered the horse to a boulder in a hollow, leaving Fellah to remain on guard.

The smaller buildings were the workers' quarters. Behind was a steel windmill above an artesian well, and a water-tower. That water made life possible. Everything else, every ounce of food, had to be brought in by the same lorries which took out the phospate.

The building on the hill was a bungalow, undoubtedly the residence of Von Wagen. There were a number of outbuildings, but nothing that was not absolutely essential. It was a place for work only.

Polskie pointed to the light in the bungalow.

"They will be there!" he said confidently, and his fists tightened into bony hammers.

"Careful!" warned Aly, as they crept up the narrow path. "They are many, and they are armed."

"Give me back the gun!" growled the Pole, holding out his hand.

This Aly refused to do, and Polskie did not persist. So far he had submitted to Aly's leadership without question.

They approached the building cautiously, crawling the last part of the way until they were beneath the lighted window.

Inside they heard loud voices and the bellow of laughter, mingled with the clinking of glasses. They peered over the bottom level of the window, which was covered by a slatted screen.

It was a large room, running the full length of the bungalow, but furnished with Spartan simplicity. Sergeant Hummel and the rest of the deserters were there, as well as a florid-faced man who must have been Von Wagen. There were chairs for only four, the others sprawled on the floor.

Von Wagen was almost as big as Polskie, but he had run to fat. His stomach bulged over the top of his belt, and he had heavy jowls. He was completely bald, with amazingly thick eyebrows. When he laughed the room shook.

A meal had been eaten recently, but the remains had not been cleared away. Von Wagen was not particular about such things.

Aly could not understand the talk, but his companion could, and was getting more and more angry. He was kneeling up, muttering under his breath. He was beginning to get out of hand. The sight of his ex-comrades lolling in there infuriated him beyond endurance. He was remembering how they had left him senseless in the blazing heat of the Saharan sun.

"Give me the gun, and I will shoot Hummel!" he hissed.

Aly moved away from him, keeping a hand on the revolver.

"It would be foolish!" he whispered. "If you killed the

sergeant the others would shoot you down the next moment. Besides, he has something that I want." He was still confident that Hummel carried the Caid's jewels. "Wait until they sleep."

Polskie grumbled, but became silent. Von Wagen had lurched to his feet, and nodded towards an inner room. He was saying that he was going to bed, and that they should all get some sleep. When he went out he closed the door behind him.

The sergeant pulled two of the chairs together and made himself comfortable, leaving the others to arrange themselves as they wished. There was a good deal of talking in low voices, and Polskie suddenly growled: "Tomorrow they go to Tunisia hidden in the lorries. We must deal with them tonight."

Aly gazed at the empty desert, and licked dry lips. He was wondering how they could best handle the situation. If only the soldiers would arrive from Biskra! With a half-crazy man beside him, he felt nervous and uncertain. He began to think he had taken too much upon himself.

Someone put out the light in the bungalow. Polskie sighed with satisfaction, and turned towards the doorway. Aly clutched at his clothing, and demanded: "What are you going to do?"

The Pole jerked a thumb towards the door, and grinned.

"It is not locked!"

"Come back!" insisted Aly, grabbing at him again. "They will not be asleep yet. Wait!"

It was a mistake to go too close, for the next moment Polskie had snatched the revolver and gripped him by the throat with one hand, lifting him off his feet and shaking him gently as he murmured in his ear: "Keep out of this! Leave everything to me."

Choking for breath, Aly could only stare into those

wide, blue eyes as he was set down on his feet. As a demonstration of what the Pole could have done, it was terribly convincing. Aly had been helpless. He had never before felt such strength. In that grip he had been unable to stir a muscle. The slightest extra pressure of those fingers would have squeezed the life out of him. A blow from one of those mighty fists could have smashed his skull.

He fingered his bruised throat and watched as Polskie crouched low against the door, listening to the mumbling of those who were still awake. He was waiting for them to settle down.

Aly could do nothing to stop him. He looked back at the desert and saw lights moving in the distance, five of them. He stared for some moments before he realized that they must be headlights. The vehicles were too far away for him to hear them, but he knew they must be caterpillar-tracked, otherwise they would not be travelling where there were no roads. The only tracked vehicles that he knew belonged to the military. This was a patrol at last.

Then he saw that the lights were not heading for Oued Zarba. They would pass some miles to the north, on the direct route to the border.

He groaned with disappointment, and as he did so there was a scuffle behind him, followed by a bellow of rage. He swung around.

A white-clad figure had leaped onto the Pole's back and pulled him down in a sitting position away from the doorway. It was either a night watchman or one of the workers who had been prowling around and seen the crouching listener outside the bungalow.

Polskie rose under the weight of the man and hurled him away with such force that he hit the wall of an outhouse and slid to the ground, dazed and helpless.

But the noise had been heard. Within the bungalow there were loud shouts, and the light came on.

"Polskie—come!" gasped Aly, but as the door was thrown open the Pole dived headlong into those about to emerge.

He did not use the revolver. Probably he had dropped it when he had been attacked, but he went in like a charging bull, carrying all before him.

The sergeant shouted something hoarsely, then the bungalow shook to the violence of the struggle. Polskie was seeing red. Bare-handed he was taking on everyone.

Aly was too scared to move. He stared through the slats over the window, hardly able to believe that one man could put up such a fight. Nobody dared shoot for they were too close together. The Pole gripped, crushed, and hurled his opponents in all directions.

The scant furniture was smashed. Von Wagen appeared in the inner doorway, revolver in hand, his face pale with dismay.

Twice Polskie went down, and each time he swept the legs of his attackers from under them and surged to his feet. Two of his opponents lay motionless, stunned or crippled. Hummel was bellowing orders that nobody could carry out.

The Pole's objective was the sergeant. Finally he hurled the others from his path, and dived on Hummel.

Hummel raised his revolver to fire at point-blank range, but Polskie swept the weapon aside with one huge hand, and the bullet narrowly missed Von Wagen, who was edging into the room. Then the Pole's hand was on Hummel's throat.

The sergeant went limp, the gun dropped from his hand, and he doubled at the knees. A few seconds more, and his neck would have been broken, but Von Wagen, coming up behind, brought down the butt of his heavy revolver on the maddened giant's head.

Polskie fell back against the wall, and slid to the floor,

dragging Hummel down with him. The Pole was unconscious. The sergeant extricated himself and staggered to his feet, his face deathly white.

"Tie him up!" he croaked. "We'll deal with him later."

Aly did not understand the words, but he saw Hummel's expression, and saw men leap on Polskie and twist his arms behind his back. He felt sure that the Pole was doomed, and that he would share his fate if he lingered.

He ran from the bungalow as shouts came from the workers' quarters. They were coming to see what was happening. Aly did not let himself be seen. The Pole had spoiled everything. Now the only hope was to try and intercept the patrol.

He ran to the hollow where he had left his four-legged friends. Fellah was whining anxiously. Okba was stamping and snorting.

The headlights of the desert patrol were now two miles away, heading east. They were bound for the border area. They had been told to seal off the frontier.

"Steady!" breathed Aly, as he tightened the girths of the impatient stallion.

He gained the saddle as Okba bounded forward, and had barely time to settle himself before the excited horse was galloping northwards, anxious to get away from the uproar.

It required all Aly's strength to wrench Okba's head round to the east, then he lay forward and shut his mind to thoughts of obstacles or falls as he let the stallion have its way. Fellah loped as silently as a ghost a few yards in the rear.

The patrol cars had a big start, but they could make no more than twenty miles an hour over that rough country. That it was very rough was proved by the way the headlights one moment shone towards the sky, and the next at the ground. Okba could make a better average speed under such conditions.

Aly could not see the ground over which he was speeding. The cool night air almost whipped the turban from his head. It cut through his thin garments and strained to lift him from the saddle, but he sat tight, feeling that Okba's hoofs touched the ground only rarely.

It was a reckless ride, and in daylight he would not have galloped over such a surface. Ridges alternated with gullies, deep sand with shale. Only a desert-bred horse could have kept its footing. Only a tough Arab breed could have avoided a broken leg. Neither did the saluki drop far behind.

"Faster! Faster!" breathed the boy, and Okba stretched his neck and drank the wind into his flaring nostrils.

They were catching up with the patrol. They could hear the roar of the powerful motors as the tracks churned up sand and stones. They could see five squat, moving shapes.

Aly shouted, but his voice was drowned by the noise of the vehicles. Once Okba stumbled almost to his knees, and Aly was thrown against the high pommel of the saddle so hard that his stomach was almost caved in. He was left without breath to shout any more.

Somehow he hung on. Very soon startled faces were peering from the rearmost of the patrol cars as a white stallion came alongside and a crouching figure on its back tried to wave them to a halt.

"It is an Arab—a boy—and a dog!" yelled someone, and an officer gave the order for the patrol to halt.

Okba skidded to a standstill. Aly lay over the saddle pommel and retched. Then he drew a deep breath and blinked into the blinding glare of a searchlight which had been swivelled to shine upon him.

"Who are you? What do you want?" demanded a voice.

Okba reared away from the light.

"Sidi, turn it off!" gasped Aly. "I have news. The men you seek—the deserters—are at Oued Zarba. They shot down your flying-machine. They are going to kill someone who was helping me. You must hasten, Sidi, for soon they go to Tunisia. Please hurry!"

Men in uniform came forward and held the stallion's bridle. Aly blurted out his story while Fellah lay down with lolling tongue.

He knew they had found friends who would help them.

16 Polskie's Revenge

The five patrol cars were making full speed for Oued Zarba, but they were not travelling fast enough for Aly.

Despite their caterpillar-tracks, they could not cover the rough ground as quickly as Okba. The stallion kept forging ahead to get away from the noise of the open exhausts. The din was ear-shattering. Aly did not hear the officer who shouted for him to come back. Fellah panted close behind.

Under such conditions a good horse could out-distance any mechanical vehicle. It could leap gullies, whereas the trucks either had to find a way around or take them very slowly. Loose stones clogged the tracks, but Okba spurned them with flailing hoofs. He was eager to get away from the roaring monsters, with their foul breath of oily fumes.

Aly did not deliberately speed up the stallion, but he found himself half a mile in front of the patrol, and he did not wait for them. He was anxious to get back to the phosphate mine to see what was happening.

He thought of the big, slow-witted Pole whose impetuousness had precipitated this crisis. Polskie was probably dead by now, and Aly hoped that his captors had not treated him too badly.

There was shouting and confusion around the mine buildings when they reached there. The workers were panicking. Von Wagen was not there to give them orders.

Okba could not be checked until he was among the huts. Someone shouted, and tried to grab the bridle. The stallion reared, and one of its hoofs caught the man on the head. He dropped.

"Keep back!" yelled Aly. "You have nothing to fear. Where are the foreigners?"

He heard someone trying to start a lorry, and turned in that direction. Von Wagen was in the driving seat, bellowing at an Arab who was vainly swinging the starting handle. The lorry remained lifeless.

Hummel and the others were not to be seen. Aly noticed that the other truck was out of action—jacked up with one wheel missing. The vehicle had been under repair, and had been left like that all night. This meant that there was no way in which the deserters could get away on wheels.

Lights blazed in the bungalow, and a voice came hoarsely from within. Aly rode over and dismounted, tying Okba to a post.

The slatted screen had been partially torn from the window. He was able to see into the room, and could not at first understand what was swinging to and fro across his line of vision.

It was Polskie. The deserters had hung him up by his wrists to a cross-beam which ran the length of the room. He dangled with his feet clear of the floor. His face was crimson, and his veins were swollen.

The leading car was roaring up the slope, no more than a hundred yards away. The frightened Arab workers were fleeing into the desert. Von Wagen, who gave up trying to start the lorry, was running towards the mine shaft, carrying a small handbag.

The dangling Pole bellowed louder than ever. Aly hesitated no longer, but clambered through the window, unsheathing his knife.

Polskie saw and recognized him. Aly righted a chair,

climbed on it, and slashed at the cords which held the man to the beam.

Polskie dropped heavily on his feet, staggered, then got his balance. Aly cut the remaining cords from his swollen wrists. The Pole had not been hanging there very long, but already his hands were purple and puffy. He rubbed them together as he plied Aly with questions. Where were the deserters? Had they escaped? Who were those arriving outside?

Aly answered as best he could, marvelling that Polskie seemed so little hurt.

"They did not get away in the lorries," he said, as shouts came from nearby. Men were scrambling from the patrol cars. Searchlights blazed. "I saw Von Wagen running for the mine shaft."

"That is where they will be!" exclaimed Polskie, and he turned around as a young French officer appeared in the doorway, revolver in hand, two of his men close behind him.

"*Arretez!* What goes on here?" he demanded.

He was speaking to Aly, who was pressed back against the wall, but it was Polskie who replied with a burst of violence that took the Frenchman by surprise.

He had been standing with one hand on the back of the chair which Aly had used. With a jerk of his wrist he hurled it at the head of the officer, who threw up an arm to protect himself and stepped back on the toes of the man behind.

There was a bellow of pain from the soldier, a sharp report from the lieutenant's revolver as it put a shot through the roof, and Polskie leaped through the window, carrying with him the remnants of the slatted screen.

There was uproar as he charged through the group of men who had come from the truck. Before they could recover, he had dived behind one of the outbuildings and was lost in the darkness.

"Who was that? Why were you with him? Where are the men we seek?" demanded the officer, grabbing Aly by an arm.

"Sidi, he—I found him tied by his arms to that beam. I cut him down. He was the man who had been helping me—the Pole."

"And where are the others?"

"I do not know, Sidi. They had gone before I arrived, but Von Wagen ran towards the mine shaft," gasped Aly, wriggling to free his arm.

The lieutenant slowly released his grip, and shouted orders. Men ran to take up positions around the mine buildings.

Aly followed the officer outside. A corporal shouted that the Pole had gone up the hillside. A burst of shooting came from the direction of the mine.

"They have taken refuge there!" grunted the young officer, and he ordered two of the trucks to go forward.

As they crept along the foot of the hill, churning up the white dust, the patrol followed, and Aly was not far behind them. Things were now out of his hands.

When they were in position the patrol cars turned their searchlights on the tunnel from which the shots had come.

Caught in the dazzling beam of light was a crawling shape. It was Polskie, and he was worming his way towards the shaft. He did not look round, but rolled onto the narrow rail track which led to the tunnel mouth, and got behind one of the empty trolleys.

"Come back, or we fire!" warned the lieutenant. "We see you! Come back!"

Polskie took no notice. He could no longer be seen. Aly wriggled behind a boulder, and watched what followed. He wanted to ask the soldiers not to shoot Polskie, but he did not dare. They thought the Pole wanted to join the others in the tunnel. Aly knew differently. All Polskie wanted was to get his hands on Sergeant Hummel.

One of the trucks started up the slope, but became bogged down in the soft mass of phosphate which formed the surface.

The officer moved up behind it, and bellowed: "You in the tunnel—come out and surrender! It's your last chance."

There was no reply. From where he lay Aly could see that Polskie was still under the line of trolleys. He was uncoupling one of them. The soldiers could not see him.

"Come out and surrender!" repeated the lieutenant.

Again there was no reply. Aly had lost sight of Polskie.

The officer gave another order, and men followed him up the incline, fanning out, trying to take cover.

From the tunnel mouth came the splutter of Sten guns and the crack of rifles. Two soldiers were hit, and rolled down the slope. The others threw themselves flat.

The deserters meant to make a fight for it. The officer yelled angrily, and both patrol cars opened fire with their machine guns. The mouth of the tunnel was hidden in a cloud of dust.

Aly winced at the noise, but wriggled nearer. It was not every day that he had a chance to watch a battle. He would have plenty to tell Selim and the others when he got back to Yelten.

A small object came whirling out of the dust cloud, landed near the bottom of the slope, and exploded with tremendous force. This time the cloud of dust that rose was sufficient to blot out the entire scene, and as someone screamed in pain, the officer roared: "They've got grenades! Keep up the machine gun fire!"

The patrol cars were within two hundred feet of the tunnel, and poured in streams of bullets. No one could have come out and lived, but those inside had no intention of trying. They lobbed out more grenades, and one of these exploded beneath a truck, rocking it wildly. A man jumped out and ran away.

For more than five minutes the duel continued, and Aly was almost choked by the drifting dust and smoke. He knew he ought to seek a safer spot, but he was fascinated by this fight to the death, and he wanted to know what happened to Sergeant Hummel, whom he still believed carried the Caid's jewels.

Seeing that they were achieving nothing, the officer ordered one of the cars to attempt to reach the tunnel mouth, but it stalled near the top, and slid backwards, out of control.

Firing stopped, and the dust had a chance to settle. A shout went up when in the glare of the searchlights the soldiers saw one of the empty trolleys moving along the track towards the mine. To them it looked fantastic, but from where Aly lay to one side, he could see Polskie bent almost double, pushing the trolley before him. He was using it as a shield against the bullets which came from those in the mine. Aly could hear them thudding on the steel plating. Polskie ignored them, and went on pushing.

The lieutenant realized what was happening, and cried: "That madman will get himself killed, but he is keeping them busy. Now is our chance!"

He started up the hillside, and some of his men followed him, keeping out of the searchlight beam. Those in the tunnel were now concentrating all their fire on the moving trolley. They did not know who was behind it, but they knew that it represented danger. Slowly but surely it drew nearer.

Aly was so overcome with excitement that he left the shelter of the boulder and scrambled farther up the steep incline to get a better view. The climax was approaching. The soldiers were getting into a position from which they could make a final rush. Polskie still drew the deserters' fire.

The searchlights probed deep into the tunnel. Aly could

see crouching figures. Hummel could be heard encouraging his companions.

Now the trolley was almost in the tunnel entrance. There the track was level, and the Pole straightened up to yell:

"I am coming to get you, Franz Hummel!"

Aly did not understand the words, but the lieutenant did, and ordered his men to remain where they were as they watched the final act of the drama.

A hail of bullets spattered the trolley. Many of them ricocheted from the steel sides and whined along the hillside. Several passed close to Aly, who had risen to his knees to see what the Pole was doing.

Polskie was crawling beneath the trolley. All firing had ceased. Those in the mine were reloading.

Then the Pole suddenly came out below the front end of the trolley, crouching low as he charged, his big hands outstretched.

Someone stepped out in front of him, only a dozen paces away, holding a sub-machine gun at hip level. It was Hummel, and Aly saw him clearly in the white light that flooded the tunnel. His face was a mask of white dust in which two eyes gleamed. He slowly squeezed the trigger and the stream of bullets stopped Polskie as though he had run into a brick wall, but he did not go down.

The sergeant laughed hoarsely as he fired another burst. The stricken man swayed but prevented himself from falling by clutching at one of the posts that supported the roof.

Aly saw his face as he tightened his arms around the timber. He heaved with all his remaining strength.

In the silence that followed Hummel's burst of firing there came the sound of a great crack, then a loud yell from the sergeant as he plunged forward.

He was too late. Polskie threw himself backwards, still hugging the stout post. It came with him, and with it came the cross-timbers which held up the tunnel roof.

It was like watching something on a brilliantly lit

screen. The roof sagged. Hummel made a desperate effort to get past the dying giant, but a mass of rock descended on the men and hid them from view. There was a dull rumble as a section of the roof collapsed. A dense cloud of dust erupted from the entrance and hovered over the hill-side, blotting out everything.

Aly found himself coughing and spluttering. He heard the shouts of the soldiers, followed by the noise of loose boulders bouncing down the hillside, then a flying stone hit him on the head, and all went dark.

17 Aly Comes Home

Dawn was breaking with its usual triumphant blaze when Aly stirred. Something was touching his face. He raised his hand and felt the furry head of Fellah.

He opened his eyes and blinked at the dog.

"Where are we?" he murmured, fondling one silk-fringed ear. "Something has happened to my head—!"

He sat up, tenderly fingering the bump which the flying stone had caused despite the protection of his turban. The stone lay nearby, and sight of it caused him to recall everything. He had been unconscious no great length of time.

Shakily he raised himself to his feet, and looked along the hillside.

A number of soldiers were digging in the mouth of the tunnel, and were being helped by some of the Arabs who had been rounded up for the purpose. The lieutenant stood outside, directing operations, and the trucks were still at the foot of the slope.

The cool morning air rapidly cleared Aly's head. He realized that the diggers were trying to discover if anyone still lived within the shaft. It was possible that only a portion of the roof had fallen, and that some of the deserters were trapped, unharmed, beyond the fall. The rescuers had already dug in a considerable distance.

Aly was covered with dust and had a trickle of blood

down his forehead, but he was not aware of this. He walked along the hillside, Fellah trotting at his heels.

The officer heard him coming, looked up in surprise, and exclaimed: "Hullo, boy, where have you been? We missed you."

Aly's eyes went to the two tarpaulin-covered figures lying on one side of the tunnel mouth. A lot of timber and rubble had been removed from the shaft.

"I was hit by a flying stone," he explained. "Are they all dead, Sidi?"

The lieutenant motioned to the two covered shapes.

"The first two—the Pole and the sergeant—are very dead, but we have hopes for the others. We can hear voices." He patted his tunic where it bulged. "I think we have found what you sought—on the body of the sergeant—a large quantity of money and jewellery."

Aly started forward impulsively.

"That will be the Caid's. I told you about it. I—"

"Yes, it will be your Caid's, but it is safe with me. I will hand it over to him at Yelten. Meantime go down to the bungalow and rest."

As he finished speaking there were shouts behind him, and he went back into the tunnel. The rescuers had broken through, and the survivors had been contacted.

A few minutes later they staggered out, six white figures, more like ghosts than men. One of them was Von Wagen. They were all in bad condition, but thankful to be alive.

Aly watched them being given water, then remembered that Okba would be thirsty. He snapped his fingers at the saluki.

"Come, Fellah!" he said, and they went down the hill together.

Soon he was leading Okba towards the water point, where the other horses were gathered. They met the lieutenant and his men bringing in their prisoners.

"I thought I told you to rest!" said the officer, eyeing the stallion with approval. "So this is the horse you were riding! Does it belong to your Caid?"

"No, Sidi, it is mine!" Aly told him, proudly. "It is the finest horse in North Africa."

The lieutenant smiled.

"Then see that it is fed and watered, for you both did a good job last night. But for you we would have continued to the border, and these ruffians would have escaped."

There was very little food for horses in the mining camp, and most of it had been shared out among the other horses, but Okba was not a fussy eater and was content with dates and brown beans, which Aly obtained by rifling one of the store sheds.

"When we get back to Yelten you will have the finest feed possible!" he promised his companions, as he found something for himself and Fellah.

Only when he had made the horse comfortable and had tended Fellah's sore feet, did he curl up on some sacking.

Fellah crept up beside him, and lay full length against his back. They both slept.

It was sunset three days later when Aly rode into the oasis of Yelten at the head of a small cavalcade.

At his side ran Fellah, limping only slightly. Behind came the horses which had been stolen from the Caid's stable. They were ridden by some of the men from the patrol.

The return ride had taken two days, one night having been spent in the ruined fort at Bella, where helicopters had dropped supplies.

Now was the moment of Aly's triumph. As he appeared at the top of the wadi, Okba proudly tossing his heavy mane and swishing his long tail, men, women, and children ran out from under the palms to greet him.

"Aly is back ! Greeting, Aly!" they cried.

Leading the runners came Mamounah, her round face flushed and beaming. She rushed at Okba, leaped lightly with one foot on her brother's, and a moment later was up in front of him, sharing the plaudits of the crowd.

"My brother, we are all happy that you have returned safely!" she whispered. "The Caid wishes to see you at once."

"The Caid? Is he not in hospital in Biskra?"

"He was brought back yesterday and is in bed in his own house. A French officer called on him and returned his jewels, but we all know it was you who recovered them."

Aly shook his head, dizzy from the acclamation. Men reached up to shake his hand, and the women gave their high-pitched ululation, working their fingers rapidly to and fro over their lips. To add to the din, Fellah began to bark, then out of the throng sprang Selim, eyes wide with happiness as he shouted up to his friend: "Greeting, Aly! My donkey has come back."

Aly waved to him. He knew he would soon hear the story of the donkey's return from Ain Zara, but first he must obey the Caid's summons.

Some of the horses whinnied with pleasure when they saw their stables again. It had been a hard and terrible time for them, but now they would be able to rest and regain their former condition.

Selim was still at Aly's side, and as Aly dismounted and helped his sister to the ground, the donkey boy said: "Leave Okba to me! I will see that he gets the best."

Finding it hard to believe that all this was happening to him, Aly entered the big, white house, where the servants greeted him with smiles, and hurried him to the cool chamber where the pale, convalescent Caid lay among many cushions.

"Peace be with you, Sidi!" murmured Aly, and went down on one knee to kiss the hand extended to him, but

Ramdan ben Mizan gripped his shoulder and pulled him up beside him.

"And peace be with you, Aly!" he smilingly replied. "It is good to see you. I hear that you have been running Yelten in my absence!"

Aly blushed, and stammered: "Sidi, I did not mean —I—"

"Whether you meant it or not you have done well—as well as I could have done," said the Caid. "The officer who was here yesterday told me much about you, and I am very proud that you are in my service. He also gave me back my family jewels, and told me I must thank you for their recovery."

"I went to find Mamounah—" explained Aly. "When I learned that the sergeant had your jewels, I followed to keep an eye on him."

The Caid patted his forearm.

"The officer told me differently. He said that but for you these men would have escaped to Tunisia, and my jewels would have gone with them. It will take me a long time to repay you for all you have done, Aly ben Rabah, but rest assured that I shall do so. What was that noise I heard when you arrived? Have you brought an army with you?"

"We brought back your horses, Sidi."

The Caid raised both hands in mock despair.—

"Okba—he is safe?" he asked.

"Safe and well, Sidi. But for him none of these things could have happened."

The Caid shook his head.

"It was the will of Allah! Now go and join your family. They will be awaiting you. Tell them that as long as Ramdan ben Mizan lives, they will never want. Tell your mother that she should be proud of her son, and that I would be proud if he were my own."

Still very weak, the Caid fell back among the cushions